ASSASSINS
INCORPORATED

Phillip Drayer Duncan

Assassins Incorporated
Phillip Drayer Duncan
Second Edition Copyright © Phillip Drayer Duncan, 2016

Published by Yard Dog Press at Create Space

This is a work of fiction. Names, characters, places, and incidents are the products of the author's imagination or are used fictitiously and are not to be construed as real. Any resemblance to actual events, locales, organizations, or persons, living or dead, is entirely coincidental.

ISBN 978-1-945941-01-6
Assassins Incorporated
Second Edition Copyright © Phillip Drayer Duncan, 2016

Yard Dog Press
710 W. Redbud Lane
Alma, AR 72921-7247

http://www.yarddogpress.com

Edited by Selina Rosen
Copy & Technical Editor Lynn Rosen
Cover art by Mitchell Bentley

First Edition July 1, 2014
Second Edition October, 2016
Printed in the United States of America
0 9 8 7 6 5 4 3 2 1

DEDICATION

This book is dedicated to my mother.
Mom, if you read this book... Don't... Just don't.
Love ya!

ACKNOWLEDGEMENT

A big special thank you to Selina Rosen for taking the time to work with me, for answering my stupid questions, and trying to teach me. There was so much red ink on the first copy of this manuscript that it looked like a murder scene. It was hard to tell if she was actually editing or using my manuscript as a cutting board to gut fish. But seriously, she put a lot of time and patience into not only polishing this story but in teaching me. The only problem is that now her voice is stuck in my head every time I edit. Of course, there's much worse voices you could have in your head when you're editing. Thank you, Selina.

CHAPTER ONE

People are stupid, thought **Rharo Staris,** *that's why it's so easy to take their money.* He smiled thinking about the rich old man and his fat wife. They were gullible and they had more money than they knew what to do with. Their greed drove them to try to attain yet more through gambling. It had been too easy for him. In fact, it was always too easy. Casinos were full of suckers. Rharo could attest to that simply by the fact that he had been hiding out in the great Notaris Flivarium Casino for over a month, sleeping in presidential suites and hadn't spent any of his own money yet.

He took a sip from his fruity beverage and glanced around the machines, always keeping an eye out for the next mark. By now the casino was on to him, but there was nothing that they could do. No, he was too careful for that. He was too good. He lost track of all of the scams he had run, but he always came out squeaky clean in the end. Yeah the casino knew, but as long as he didn't screw the house, he didn't figure they cared. After all, he was a paying customer.

Rharo laughed to himself, and pressed the button to make the digital slot machine spin again. The slot machines were a silly human invention and rather boring. He was losing his mark's money quickly, but he didn't care. He would find another. At this point, he was so bored with gambling, that the only fun he had was in his minor scams. The spaceport casino had all of the luxury it boasted and then some. He still remembered when the big push began for the casinos to open in deep space as a way to avoid civil law. Most planetary governments hadn't started claiming the dead space in their systems as sovereign territory until the past few years. Out here, the casinos could run by their own laws for the most part. Thus, casinos like Notaris Flivarium offered drugs, prostitution, and other services that were mostly illegal planet side. They still had their own red tape to deal with, though. That was one of the reasons that he had decided to hide here.

He shook his head and took another drink. Everything had gone wrong back on Maestrom. One botched heist and suddenly he owed a lot of money to a lot of powerful people; a lot more money than he could make by running scams in a casino.

Now he was stuck in this floating casino because it was one of the places off limits to the Bounty Hunter's Association. The hunters knew he was here, too, but because they had never set up an agreeable contract with The Notaris Flivarium Casino, they couldn't do business here. So as long as he was here he was safe, but he would be trapped here forever if he didn't think of a scheme to make enough money to pay his debts.

He glanced over and caught a set of tall tentacle eyes staring at him from a few machines over. He glanced down toward the face and realized that it was a Vantegee female. He knew enough about the species to know she was middle aged, and the gown she wore indicated she was wealthy. She smiled at him. He smiled back and forced his blue-skinned cheeks to redden into a purple shade. Her smile broadened.

He wasn't sure why, but many Vantegee woman always found Rharo's species attractive. Like most of the males of his species, he had light blue skin, soft features, bright orange hair, and crimson eyes. Everyone knew the Selu race was attractive, and he definitely had no problem boasting that he was exceptional amongst his handsome race.

Glancing over again, he could tell that the woman was into him. He, on the other hand, found Vantegee women repulsive. They were far too thin and their skin was an ashy grey. Beyond that, who wanted to get in bed with a woman that had tentacle eyes? Still, she would be an easy mark, and he would be happy to take her money. Sacrifices had to be made to turn a buck.

A shadow fell over him, and before he could turn around the voice of a human male said, "Rharo Staris."

Humans… Rharo hated humans. They were his least favorite species. They were the newest species to the galactic community, having only been around fifty years or so, and they were always a pain. They were ugly creatures, too. He wished the whole species would have just stayed on their little Earth planet and out of galactic business.

He turned to face the human and flashed his best smile. The figure that stood before him was decked out in battle-scarred, gun-metal grey armor. It was a cheap, common armor worn by half the mercs in space. The human had a large assault rifle strapped to his back, a laser pistol on his hip, and an assortment of knives and grenades strapped around his body. The armor and every bit of his gear looked like it had passed through some hard years and several different owners. A bounty hunter on a budget. Rharo knew the type all too well.

His helmet was round and fairly plain in design but had been customized. Much of the custom paint had been chipped, or perhaps blasted away, but he vaguely recognized the design. He wasn't familiar with Earth's zoology, but the face plate was intended to look like a serpent of some species. The helmet's eyes were slitted and glowing with a dull blue light. The vague lines of a hand-painted mouth were barely visible, but the long, white fangs painted down the sides of the face plate were clear.

He had to hand it to the human; he looked intimidating enough to scare most cheap thugs.

Rharo continued spreading his smile and said, "I'm sorry, but I'm afraid you've got the wrong person. My name is Vish..."

"No. Your name is Rharo Stairs, the petty criminal and scam artist that owes a lot of dangerous people money."

Rharo raised an eyebrow. "I can assure you sir..."

"Hiding like a coward..."

"Sir, I most certainly..."

"Scamming people in a casino to get by..."

"That's not me. I'm a legitimate business man..."

"With delusions of grandeur," the human said. "That pretty much sums it up right?"

Rharo glared at him. "Fine, human. I am Rharo Staris. Renown throughout the galaxy. Now be a good little errand boy and go away. Your armor smells."

"Renown." The human chuckled to himself. "If being hated by everyone that you owe money to or have cheated is being renown, well that's certainly you."

Rharo chuckled, turned back to his slot machine, and pressed the button to spin it again. A moment later he glanced over his shoulder and said, "You're still here? I thought I told you to leave. Do I need to have security escort you out for harassing a paying customer?"

"It's not going to be that easy, Rharo."

Rharo turned around again and made an effort of laughing right in the man's armored face. "Actually it is, human. You see, in case you didn't know, The Notaris Flivarium Casino doesn't have a contract with you Bounty Hunters, so other than annoying me, there's nothing you can do."

Rharo glanced down as the armored human slowly drew the

pistol from his hip. The man said, "Actually Rharo, you're quite wrong. See you in hell."

Rharo laughed at the man's bluff. "I'm a Selu, human. Even the most common religions of my species don't believe in your human hell, bounty hunter."

"It's... It's a saying you jackass," the human said, his voice giving away that he was younger than Rharo might have expected. "And you're wrong."

Again deciding to play out the bluff, Rharo asked, "About what?"

"I'm not a bounty hunter," the human said. "My name is Agkistrodon, and I'm with Assassins Incorporated, and we do have a contract with The Notaris Fliv... However you say it... Casino."

"What?" Rharo said. "But surely they wouldn't send assassins. I owe too much money to be killed!"

The armored human shrugged. "I guess the people you are indebted to gave up on getting a return on their investment."

Before Rharo could argue further, there was a bright flash of light, and then all was darkness for Rharo Staris.

CHAPTER TWO

"You honestly don't see what I'm upset about?"

"I honestly don't," Agkistrodon replied. "I thought you would be happy. You are the one that said you were losing customers to Rharo's scams, and having him gone would relieve a great burden from your shoulders, and that you were good with me taking him out in the casino. I had a legit contract to come end the guy's life, you approved me doing it here, and it's done. So really, I did you a favor. Problem solved."

The casino floor manager stared at him for a few moments. He was a short, chunky creature covered in hair. Agkistrodon wasn't sure what species. His long ears twitched a few times, and then he began screaming again. "You killed him in the middle of the floor! All of the customers saw! That's not what we agreed to! When my boss finds out I'm going to get fired! I knew I shouldn't have let you go after this guy in the casino! Even if you had a perfectly legitimate contract!"

Agkistrodon waived the notion away. "You are being over dramatic."

"You killed a man in the middle of the casino! There is blood everywhere! Blood on the machines! Blood on the floor! There was even blood on customers! You shot him right in front of everyone!"

Agkistrodon shrugged. "I'm an assassin."

"Yeah!" the floor manager cried. "You are supposed to kill people in stealth. I thought you would poison his drink! Choke him while he slept! Or take him away from people and shoot him! Not kill him in the middle of my casino!"

The floor manager sighed with defeat and stared at the floor. "Do you know how hard I worked to get where I'm at? And it's over. When upper management finds out that I allowed an assassin to kill someone in the middle of the game floor I'm done."

"You're looking at it all wrong. You've got to play up the positive side."

"What could possibly be positive about this!?"

"Well," Agkistrodon said, "when they ask you about it show some confidence, puff out your furry little chest, and say something about how you were taking the initiative to show thieves how the casino responds to scum bags that scam their valued customers."

"You think that would really work?" the floor manager asked, showing the slightest glimmer of hope.

"Of course," Agkistrodon said. "They won't fire you. Hell, if you play it right it they might promote you. Tell them this is great PR. The customers will know that your casino takes security seriously, and criminals would think twice about messing with your customers. It's a win win really."

"That might work," the floor manager replied while rubbing his chin thoughtfully. "Okay, I'll give it a try."

"You're welcome," Agkistrodon said.

"Now, when are you going to clean that mess up?"

The armored face stared back in silence.

"Well?"

"Don't you have cleaning bots?"

"My cleaning bots aren't made for cleaning up dead bodies!"

"I'm sure they'll do fine," Agkistrodon said as he turned and began walking out of the office. "I wish I could help you out with the mess…"

"Wait! Where are you going!?"

Agkistrodon shrugged. "Back to my ship. Job's done. I've got to go get paid, and then head on to the next one. People all over the galaxy are waiting patiently for my services."

"You can't leave this mess in my casino!"

Agkistrodon didn't bother to respond.

"Congratulations Agkistrodon, you managed to sneak in and steal our target."

He knew the voice, and in response he slowly turned around with as much casual disregard as he could muster. He had known better than to think he would get away from the casino without running into her. He should have known that she would be waiting at his ship.

"Lenis Formoon," Agkistrodon said. "It's nothing personal."

"Of course not," Lenis said. Her voice was deep and rich.

She was human, perhaps in her mid-thirties. She had gorgeous auburn hair and grey battle armor that was more dented and beat to hell than his own. She was attractive in a way, but she had never shown any interest in anything but the job. She was cold, relentless, and just stubborn enough to usually end up getting her way. Not this time though.

Lenis shook her head. "You have potential, Agkistrodon. Have you considered my offer about joining my team? I can get you compensation close to your current base salary and our commissions are similar. Your retirement can roll right over into our program."

"Becoming a bounty hunter?" Agkistrodon said. "I dunno about that, Lenis. I appreciate the offer, and I'll continue to consider it, but I've got a pretty good set up with Assassins Inc."

"Is that so?" Lenis smiled. "I have it from a reliable source that our dental plan is considerably better than yours."

Agkistrodon shrugged.

"You don't care about your teeth?"

"I do, but they're in pretty good shape. A better dental plan isn't enough to make me switch."

"Fair enough." Lenis shrugged and waived her men away from his ship. "Be careful out there. Rharo Staris owed a lot of people money. They aren't going to be too happy that he was assassinated before they had a chance to recuperate their losses."

"I was just doing a job," Agkistrodon said. "I guess the Ja-Jamalee Family on Feeintan Quarris decided they weren't as worried about getting their money back as they were about putting an end to Rharo. I was just lucky enough to be the first assassin to sign up for it."

Lenis stared back at him for a moment and let out a burst of laughter.

"What?" Agkistrodon asked.

"You took a job from someone on Feeintan Quarris?"

"Yes."

Again Lenis laughed and turned to begin walking away.

"What!?"

Lenis glanced over her shoulder, and said, "Nothing. It just seems I've overestimated your potential."

She walked away without another word.

Agkistrodon glanced around himself, but he appeared to be alone. As he stepped on to his ship he shook his head, and said, "Wonder what the hell that was about?"

CHAPTER THREE

"Yo, Brandon! How's the hunt going, man?" said the green alien face on the screen.

"Rego! Dammit!" Agkistrodon spat. "When I'm on the job its Agkistrodon! How many times do I have to tell you!? I could have a high priority client here."

Rego stared back at the screen for a moment and said, "You don't."

"Maybe I do! You don't know!"

"Yeah I do. You are alone in your ship. I know this because you are always alone in your ship. And why do you use that stupid name anyway?"

"As you know, I'm from the Ozarks back on Earth. It's one of the few areas that still has rural forest lands. Anyway, there were these serpent creatures we had to watch out for growing up. They were venomous pit vipers. Cottonmouths and Copperheads. Every kid that grew up where I'm from was afraid of them."

"So?"

"So, Agkistrodon is the scientific name for the family of snake they are from. So I thought it was kind of a cool name."

"It would be cool if there was any possible way that anyone else would get it."

"Well anyway," said Agkistrodon, whose real name was Brandon, "I have some good news."

"Oh yeah? What's that?"

Brandon removed his helmet, revealing a human face with fairly simple features. He was in his late twenties, not quite handsome, but fair. He had short brown hair and was a few days behind on shaving.

He glanced down at the helmet in his hands, the face of Agkistrodon. He tossed it aside and glanced back up at Rego. "The target has been eliminated."

"By who?" Rego asked, his four nostrils flaring out while he chuckled with delight.

"You're quite funny," Brandon said. "But seriously. I got the target. The job is done."

"So you're finally going to pay rent?"

"Congratulations, Brandon! You did it, Brandon! I'm so proud of you best friend! You should hurry home so we can celebrate," Brandon mocked, not hiding the sarcasm that was dripping from each word.

Rego glared at him and said, "Oh c'mon, you act like it's your first successful hit. Are you sure it's done and that you are getting paid? We really need to pay our rent before we get kicked out on the street."

"Not everyone can be as successful an assassin as the great Rego Halloran," Brandon growled.

Rego laughed. "See that's the problem. I'm not very successful. I'm just more successful than you, and I handle my money better so that I can make sure that I pay my bills on time, and don't make my roommate cover my half. If I were successful I wouldn't need to share a dingy apartment with you, and I wouldn't need to share a dingy dock with you. And if you are joking about completing this job and getting paid, then I might not even have that because we are almost surely going to lose the apartment. So please tell me you really are getting paid."

"Calm down, Rego," Brandon replied. "I'm getting paid. I've already notified the client that the hit is done, and they are already processing payment. If you want proof, then meet me at the dock in about an hour. They are supposed to be delivering payment then."

"And this isn't a joke?"

"No! Man, I'm serious! And this job paid fairly well, too! I should be set for a while. I'm still not sure why nobody else volunteered to take this job on, but they didn't, I did, and now I'm getting paid."

Rego paused for a moment, and asked, "Who was the client for this job?"

"The Ja-Jamalee Family on Feeintan Quarris."

"You took on a job for a Feeintanen?"

"Yes," Brandon replied. "What's the problem?"

Rego laughed and ended the connection.

Brandon sighed. Both Rego and Lenis had laughed when they heard who he was doing this job for. It was a little disconcerting, but he decided he would check his messages to make sure that payment was going through.

He had recently been able to tie his two communication accounts together, so he was able to access them from within his ship, his home, his armor, and the small watch-like device he wore when he wasn't in armor. This allowed him access to his personal Brandon Daivik account, and his professional Agkistrodon account pretty much anywhere he went. That way if someone needed to call him he was reachable, but he kept that setting to emergencies only, because the last thing he wanted was his mom calling him in the middle of a gun fight. However anyone could leave him a voice message, visual voice message, script message, or send him data at any time.

He hit the controls to have his accounts brought up on the ship screen. It appeared that he had two new voice messages on his personal account. He could have pulled up the caller's information first, but instead just pressed the play option.

He let out an audible sigh as the voice of his mother filled the ship's speaker system. "Brandon Daivik! I carried you for nine months, and spent eighteen years raising your sorry ass, the least you can do is call your mother every once in a while!"

Brandon mouthed the words along with the message.

She continued. "Anyway, did you consider what I said about going back to school? Your father and I will help you pay for it. I don't see what the issue is. I'm sending you information on several great medical schools. If you studied hard, in a few years you could be a doctor... You're twenty-seven years old, now it's time for you to grow up and get a real job. You can't work as a telemarketer your whole life."

He smiled to himself. He hadn't told his mother that he had become an assassin. He didn't think that she would take it well.

"Also, you need to call your brother. He says that you two haven't spoken in three months and that he thinks you're mad at him..."

"Damn right I am," he mumbled at the message.

"You boys are just too stubborn. Just like your father!"

"Oh yeah, because we surely didn't get that from he you," he mumbled at the recording.

"I just want you two to get along..."

He switched the message off, and said, "That's about enough of that."

The next message was from his girlfriend Naria. They had been going out for a couple of years now, but things weren't too serious. She had a good sense of humor, a brilliant personality, and was as cute as could be. The only problem was that she also worked for Assassins Incorporated and the company didn't like any conflicts of interest. She was an accountant, so it was possible they could get an exception, but it was also possible that they could get fired if it was ever discovered. The good news was that hardly anyone he worked with new him outside of his armor.

He pressed play and smiled as a video of Naria's face appeared on the screen. She was short, curvy, and had mid-length brunette hair. "Hey Brandon. I know you're working, but I just wanted to remind you that we are supposed to go out tonight. I didn't want you to forget. Love ya."

Next he moved to the messages on his Agkistrodon account. There was nothing new, just the same previous message, confirming that his payment was being processed.

"So what's the problem?" he asked out loud, but there was no one on the ship except him.

"Carrots?"

"Carrots!"

"Carrots?" Brandon repeated his question. He understood Rego's answer; he just still hadn't quite wrapped his head around it.

Rego shook his head, and pressed the release button on one of the crates. From inside he lifted out the largest carrot that Brandon had ever seen.

Brandon looked around the dock at the hundreds and hundreds of crates that were taking up literally every free inch of their small docking bay. He glanced back toward Rego and said, "So... Carrots?"

"You're an idiot," Rego said. "You never take a job from a Feentianen! Everyone knows that! They have a carrot-based economy!"

"A carrot-based what?" Brandon asked. "I've never even heard of their planet till this!"

Rego shook his head, and said, "Alright, you know how when a new planet joins the galaxy there's a lot of resource and crop sharing? Well when your Earth joined the galaxy the Feentianens discovered that carrots grew exceptionally well on Feeintan Quarries." Rego waved the large carrot around. "In fact, they grew larger there than they did on your Earth. And the Feeintan's learned something else as well, your Earth carrots contained the primary nutrients they needed to survive, and the whole species loves the flavor. Carrots became the primary cash crop on Feeitan Quarris until eventually carrots became currency! Their entire economy is based around carrots. A carrot-based economy."

"A carrot-based economy," Brandon repeated thoughtfully, again looking at the stacks and stacks of crates filling the dock that he and Rego split rent on. He glanced back up at Rego. "So is there like a way we can trade this for standard currency?"

"Yeah," Rego said. "Go sell it to a grocery market! You imbecile! This is why none of the other assassins took this job! There's no money to be had!"

"So," Brandon said, "about that rent that I'm behind on..."

Rego growled. "You've got even bigger things to worry about. When word gets back to work that you took this job and got paid in carrots, you're gonna be lucky if they don't fire you for embarrassing the company. At the very best you will absolutely be the laughing stock of Assassins Inc."

"Son of a bitch."

Rego slapped him on the back and said, "And it's about to get a lot worse. We've been summoned for an emergency meeting."

"Ah crap, I was supposed to take Naria out tonight."

"She'll be at the meeting, too. They've summoned everyone. Something big is going down."

"Wow, well it's not like I can interact with her."

"True, but at least she can't hold it against you."

"Carrot-based economy," Brandon shook his head. "This week just cannot get any worse."

"Ah, c'mon now, it's possible no one else heard about this."

CHAPTER FOUR

"Cawwots!"

"Carrots..." Brandon replied.

"You got paid in cawwots!" replied his toad faced boss. It was a little hard to take him seriously at times with the way his slobber, long-tongued mouth couldn't make out R's and L's. The fact that his cheeks turned red when he was mad didn't help, either. He was a big guy, too. Big enough that he could probably crush Brandon in a single hop.

"Yeah, Garrett," Brandon replied, "I got paid in cawwots."

For a second, he thought that his supervisor's big frog eyes were gonna pop right out of their sockets, as he replied, "That's Mistew Gammon to you Agkistwodon!"

"Hey don't get mad at me because you have a first name you can't pronounce in Galactic Standard! And the company encourages us to use first names!"

"Don't tawk to me about the company! You'we vewy wucky to even stiww have a job! Do you undewstand the embawassment you've caused the company? You'we gonna be wucky if a wite up is all you get!"

Brandon sighed. "I was kind of hoping that no one would find out. How high has it made it up the chain?"

"Evewyone knows!" Gammon spat. "Diwectow Naste knows! Even Vice Pwesident Wynx Wufus has heard!"

"Vice President Lynx Rufus has heard?" Brandon repeated. "Son of a..."

"Hey! Watch it!" Gammon replied. "You'we in enough twoubwe without me having to wite you up for cuwsing, too."

"Right, sorry, I forget that the company that kills people for money doesn't like profanity" Brandon said, shaking his head. "Look, I didn't mean to make the company look bad, nor did I mean to make you look bad."

"Why wouwd you take a contwact fwom a Feeintanen? Evewyone knows not to do that!"

"I didn't! No one ever told me!"

"Evewyone knows!"

Brandon shook his helmeted head again and said, "Do you

know what they are going to do? Am I going to get fired?"

"I don't know yet. If it was my decision, then yes you would be fiwed. How many convewsations have we had to have about gwenade safety? You wefuse to pway safe with expwosives and now you puww something wike this! You should be fiwed!"

"Thanks, boss man, I appreciate your support."

"But fowtunatewy fow you, it's not my decision. Uppew management has to decide how much of an exampwe they want to set."

"Great," Brandon said. "Then I'll patiently look forward to hearing from you."

"It won't be wong. I'm suwe they wiww have a decision in the next few days. Now get back out thewe and pay attention to the meeting."

Brandon turned and headed back toward the conference room. He knew he should have counted himself lucky that Garrett Gammon hadn't made a point of berating him in front of the whole sect in the middle of the conference room. Okay, so yeah, it was his fault for getting paid in carrots, but how the hell was he supposed to know? It's not like the citizens of Feeintan Quarris advertise that carrots are their currency! Lots of planets have their own currency, but it can be easily changed to the Galactic Standard... Usually. When he had gone into the Assassin Assignment System and agreed to take on the job, it had showed the value in Galactic Standard, not in carrots. Now he was probably going to lose his job.

Back in the conference room he waded through the crowd of armored assassins and business casual employees, hearing the occasional sneers and jests as he passed by. There were approximately two thousand people in attendance, and it was more than a little disconcerting that total strangers were pointing and laughing at him. He had busted his ass for the past three years trying to be a model employee and someone promotable. Well he had finally managed to make himself a reputation within the company; too bad it was as a total jackass.

His only real hope, was that he could slide through with a write up, keep his head down, and hope that in time this whole thing would blow over. In the corporate world there is always another jackass to step into the meat grinder, and with two thousand employees in this sect of Assassins Inc. there was a good chance that someone else would do something more asinine soon. He just had to hope he didn't get fired.

He wondered what Naria would say? She was usually pretty understanding, but the idea that she knew about his monumental screw up bugged him. He hadn't seen her here yet, but with so many employees in attendance it wasn't a big surprise.

He pushed his way through the crowd until he found Rego and approached him. Rego glanced over and said, "I'm not sure I want to be seen standing beside you."

"Very funny," Brandon replied. "Some friend you are."

Rego shrugged. "This is business. Keep friendship and business separated. I don't need you ruining my reputation, too. Of course, on the other hand your reputation is so bad right now that standing beside you probably makes mine look better. You can stay."

"Thanks buddy," Brandon spat.

"No problem. So what did Garrett Gammon have to say about your ordeal?"

"Oh you know... I'ww be wucky to keep my job. If it was up to him I would be fiwed. The big wigs want to make an exampwe of me. You know, that sort of thing."

"Well," Rego said with a shrug "the good news is that you didn't use your real name to join the company, Mr. Philup Mecrevice. You could always get a new fake name, less shitty armor, a better assassin name than Agkistrodon, and try again."

"Very funny, and keep it down," Brandon said as he stifled a laugh. His real name was Brandon Daivik. Philup Mecrevice was the fake name on his personnel file though and as far as the company knew, that was his real name. Only Rego, Naria, and a handful of others he trusted knew his real name. Brandon shook his head and said, "It's not that easy. Coming up with a false identity is tricky."

"I can only imagine. How did you end up with a name like Philup Mecrevice anyway?"

Brandon shrugged. "The guy that helped me acquire my false identity is a real asshole."

"So why even bother with a fake name?" Rego asked. "Why not just use your real name?"

"I have my reasons."

"Which are?"

"None of your damn business."

"Ouch," Rego replied with a laugh, then lowering his voice said, "Oh look! There's Naja Ashei!"

Brandon was in no mood to care, but glanced over anyway.

The black-clad form of Naja Ashei was slowly working his way through the crowd. Assassins and administrative personnel were giving him plenty of room.

"You know you're a bad ass when you are in a room full of assassins and soulless corporate dicks, and everyone is moving out of your way," said Rego.

Brandon grunted in agreement.

"Naja Ashei," Rego said. "The most successful assassin in the business today. Second only to our very own sect Vice President Lynx Rufus. Naja is such a beast. If I heard that he was after me, I would just kill myself."

"Yeah," Brandon replied, while he stared at the legendary assassin. He wore lithe black armor that looked like it hadn't seen a day of combat. His head was covered with a black hood, but if you got close enough you could see the black helmeted face below, highlighted by two 'X' shaped white lights covering his eyes. Few weapons were on display on his person, but everyone knew he was a walking arsenal. The only weapons you could see clearly were the two katanas strapped on his back.

"He's so good…"

"I get it!" Brandon cut him off.

"Oh yeah, I forgot you have history. Didn't he shoot you?"

"Yeah."

"You should be proud! Not too many people can claim they were shot by Naja Ashei and lived to tell about it," Rego said. Then with a hint of excitement, "Oh man! He's looking over here."

Brandon glanced up and realized the famous assassin was staring straight at him. He held his gaze for a few moments longer, and then the legendary assassin shook his head.

Rego burst out in laughter. "Oh man! You are so screwed! Even Naja Ashei has heard about what a dumb ass you are!"

Brandon shook his head and thought about leaving, but before Rego could make fun of him anymore, Director Raxle Naste stepped on to the stage and cleared his throat, indicating that the meeting was about to begin.

Director Raxle Naste was, more or less, the second in command of their sect. Like any corporation, Assassins Incorporated had a large organizational structure. There was a President and CEO, and beneath him there were six separate sects within the galaxy. Each sect was run by a Vice President. Brandon's sect was called the Kazor Sect, and it was run by Vice President Lynx Rufus. Beneath Vice President Lynx Rufus, were several divisions, these were run by the Directors.

Director Raxle Naste was the longest-standing director, and a vile, ambitious man whose goal was obviously to get to the top, and he didn't care who he had to kill to get there. Of course, regardless of how apparent it was, in the corporate world it's all about playing the game. Director Raxle Naste would kindly tell you that his door was always open and you could approach him with anything, but if he had something to gain have no doubt that the guy would slit his own mother's throat.

Unfortunately, Raxle Naste's division was the division that Brandon fell under. Of course below the Divisions, everything was separated by department and so on, so the Director was five tiers above Garrett Gammon, Brandon's direct supervisor. He was pretty sure that Director Raxle Naste would want him to be burned at the stake for the carrots mess.

"Welcome everyone!" Director Raxle Naste said. He bore the same old red battle armor that he had worn for years, but everyone knew that he didn't do field work anymore. In his day, he was known as one of the best assassins to ever work for the company, and he liked to use himself as an example of how hard work paid off, but everyone really knew that his 'hard work' was back stabbing and ass kissing.

Raxle Naste was a human, and Brandon would guess that he was in his early to late fifties. His short-cropped, military-style hair was white, and scars zigzagged his face. There was absolutely nothing friendly about his face, and it was apparent that he had to force his beaming, fake smile.

"Glad to see so many of you in attendance for this emergency meeting. I really appreciate it. I know you all have a lot going on. It means a lot that you would take time away from your personal life to support the company."

Rego leaned closer to Brandon and whispered, "Yeah because it wasn't like it was mandatory or... Oh wait, yeah, it was."

Brandon stifled a laugh, and was thankful his smile was hidden behind his helmet.

Raxle Naste continued. "You know what it is that makes Assassins Incorporated the best corporation in the galaxy? It's family. We aren't just employees of a company; we're members of a family. We stand together through good and bad, and we take care of each other. That's what sets Assassins Incorporated apart."

It was Brandon's turn to whisper. "That's why they are trying to decide if they want to fire me for the carrots thing, because that's what family does."

Rego chuckled. "Fire you, no. The Director will probably keep you around so we all see what horrible punishment he comes up with."

"That's assuming Vice President Lynx Rufus doesn't decide to get involved," Brandon said.

"That's true," Rego said. "I wish this guy would get to the point. Blah, Blah, I'm Director Raxle Naste and I want you all to think I love you, while I'm secreting plotting on taking the Vice President's spot and am totally willing to screw you all over in the process. Blah, blah, blah."

On the stage Raxle Naste said, "I'm sure you are all wondering why we gathered you here this evening, and so it is my great honor to turn the floor over to our Vice President Lynx Rufus! Let's give our VP a big round of applause!"

The crowd cheered and clapped, which Brandon thought was quite the spectacle. The majority of employees for Assassins Incorporated were administrative. It took a lot of people to keep an assassination company in business. If Brandon had to guess, of the two thousand employees in his sect, he would say five hundred or less were actually field assassins. However, they were all present and most came dressed to in their business attire. Some dressed in battle armor, some dressed in stealth outfits, and some even dressed in business casual, but they were all dangerous. Even the administrative employees had to undergo some levels of combat training. Yet, this entire room of trained professional killers whooped and hollered for their VP just like any other corporation full of trained poodles.

Vice President Lynx Rufus stepped to the front of the stage and gave a friendly wave. He was also a human and appeared to be in his mid-fifties. His face was also covered in scars, but some were hidden under the thick, greying brown beard he wore. In place of his left eye was a protruding robotic eye that glowed with red light. He was a tall man, and he wore huge, black armor that made him look more like a walking tank than a man. The armor had quite obviously seen years of use, yet maintained a quality appearance, unlike Brandon's beat-to-hell armor. Cradled in his arm was the helmet that went with the armor, and Brandon leaned out just a little bit to try to get a better view of it. The glowing red 'V' shape of Lynx Rufus's visor was known and feared throughout the galaxy. He was, after all, the greatest assassin that had ever lived, and the heir apparent for the CEO position someday.

Rego leaned toward Brandon again and asked, "Which story do you think about the eye is true? Do you think he really plucked it out and ate it when someone tried to force him to use it to get into Assassin's INC. base back when they still used eye scanners for security? Or do you think it was shot out? Do you think the story about him hand building the replacement eye himself is true? Or do you think the company decided to build him a new one because he was such a great assassin?"

Brandon shrugged. "How the hell should I know?"

Rego shrugged. "I don't know, but I think it's neat. Lot of mystery about our VP."

"There's a lot of mystery about everyone in this business."

Rego laughed. "Yeah, like for example all the weirdoes like you that refuse to use their real names for anything. I'm sure everyone is curious about the secret identity of Agkistrodon, assassin god of carrots!"

Brandon ignored his friend and studied the face of the Vice President. Lynx Rufus didn't have that same fake smile and deceitful look in his eyes that Naste did. He had the look of a leader, a warrior.

As the cheers died down, Vice President Lynx Rufus said, "As Director Raxle Naste said, we really appreciate everyone being here for this meeting. I will keep this as brief as possible so that you can get out of here..."

The Vice President paused for a moment until the entire room became silent as death, then he went on. "A very special hit has come up. We don't know the name of the target or any other details about the target yet, but I'm being told that information is coming. What I can tell you is that this hit is going to be one of the highest-paying marks we've ever seen. The reason this target is special is that the contract for this target allows for a sect exception..."

The Vice President paused again while murmurs went up through the crowd. Typically, each sect stayed within their own territory. A contract that involved all sects was a big deal.

"... Along with that, this hit is being made public..."

The murmurs got even greater.

The VP held up his hands to silence the crowd and continued. "I know that this is unheard of. As a general rule, Assassins Incorporated doesn't compete with individuals and/or other organizations, but this time it seems that we will. This hit is going to be known throughout the galaxy, and you can rest assured that The Bounty Hunters Association will be after the target, along with every other company, mercenary, and would-be killer in the galaxy. President and CEO Domenic Voight has asked that we make a point of ensuring that Assassins Incorporated completes this hit, as it would be a huge embarrassment if we didn't."

Applause went up again, and as they finished the Vice President continued, his eyes right on Brandon. "And I am asking you, as your VP, to ensure that the Kazor Sect completes this hit! After the carrot incident we need to do this for our credibility."

"Oh man," Rego said. "The VP just called you out in front of everyone."

Brandon ignored his best friend and focused on what the VP was saying.

"Let's show the rest of the company that we're the best sect! As further encouragement, whoever succeeds in taking out the target will get one million Galactic Standard Credits, an extra two weeks of vacation, and will be a shoe-in for employee of the year! The information packet for this hit will be coming to you in the next few days. Good luck out there assassins! And make the company proud!"

A roar of applause and cheers went up.

Rego leaned closer and said, "I can't believe he mentioned the carrots. You are so screwed!"

"Maybe not. Maybe I can turn this thing around."

"Oh yeah? How do you plan to do that?"

"I'm going to be the one to take out this target!" Brandon replied.

Rego stared at him for a moment, and then started laughing. Brandon didn't care. He meant it. It was the best way to clear his name. He was going to be the one to get the target.

CHAPTER FIVE

Brandon yawned and rolled over restlessly. He had been having a dream about something, but now that he was awake he couldn't remember what. He glanced out the window and saw that it was still dark. He glanced over and saw that his communicator was blinking, indicating that he had a message of some kind. He instantly got a little excited, hoping that it might be the info on the target. First thing was first though—he had to pee. He rolled out of bed and stumbled through the dark hallway until he made it to the bathroom. As soon as he had finished his business he headed for the kitchen and poured himself a glass of water.

As he had expected, Naria had been disappointed about the cancelation of their date, but he had promised to make it up to her. Well first, he had asked her if she had wanted to come stay the night, but she had declined.

As he was midway through gulping down a glass of water, a sudden thump from another room got his attention. It wasn't exceptionally loud, it just sounded like something was knocked over. Brandon took another sip of water and said, "Rego?"

From the darkness came no reply, and he shrugged it off, assuming that Rego must have knocked something over in his sleep. Without another thought, Brandon strolled back to his room, fighting the throbbing desire to go back to sleep. He was tempted to wait until the morning to check his messages, but if it was info on the target, he wanted to know.

He scooped up his communicator and sat back down on his bed. There was another voice message from his mother, which he decided to ignore entirely. He skipped his personal stuff and went straight to his business communications, and immediately found exactly what he was looking for. The dossier for target.

He triggered the display and the information loaded up. He found himself staring at the target's name. Only it wasn't the target's name. Or at least if it was, there was some kind of problem. He read the top line again out loud, "Target Name: Brandon Daivik."

He stared at the screen a moment longer then closed his eyes, shook his tired head, and looked again.

"Brandon Daivik," he said. "That's my name. Huh, what are the odds the target would have the same name as me?"

He flipped the screen and pulled up the picture of the target. He found himself staring at a picture of his own face. Quickly he skimmed through the information. It had to be a joke. Rego maybe? But how? It came from Assassins Incorporated. It had the official seal and had required his unique code to open. It had to be real. This was a legit target dossier, and the target...Was him.

Everything they had about him was accurate, and it even included his address... He paused, remembering the crashing noise he heard while he was in the kitchen. He reached over to his nightstand and drew his laser pistol. He ensured it was loaded with a fresh battery cylinder and flipped off the safety.

Was he being paranoid? Was he losing his mind? Maybe this was just a dream! The only problem with that theory was that he wasn't waking up.

He quickly rolled off the bed and grabbed the lockbox that he kept his armor in. In a matter of moments, he was fully equipped as Agkistrodon once again. He wasn't quite sure what to do next. He glanced at the dossier again, and ran a quick search for any mention of the name Agkistrodon or Philup Mecrevice. It didn't show any matches. That was a good start. That meant that only a handful of people knew who he was. The company, including the Human Resources department had no idea that they had employee whose name was Brandon Daivik. To the company, he was Agkistrodon or Philup Mecrevice, and unless he was mistaken, he had just been hired to kill himself.

He told himself that he was being paranoid again, when he suddenly heard the footsteps coming down the hallway. If this hit was for real, then every assassin in the galaxy knew his home address. He grabbed his rifle, and pointed it at the door. A moment later the door kicked open and three armored assassins charged in. He recognized them from the company, but he didn't know their names.

They paused and stared at Brandon, and he stared back, and finally said, "It appears the target isn't here."

"We've had surveillance teams watching the house. We didn't see him leave," replied one of the assassins.

Brandon shrugged. "Well I don't see him here. I even checked under the bed, too."

The assassin nodded and asked, "How the hell did you get in here? Our team didn't see you come in."

Brandon shrugged again. "I'm sneaky. What can I say?"

He stepped past his fellow assassins and started walking toward the living room. If he was lucky he could walk right out the front door and head toward the dock. He didn't want to leave Rego sleeping while there were assassins in the house, but he certainly wasn't going to wake him up. Besides, he didn't know if he could trust Rego not to kill him. One million credits was a lot of money. So much for "family".

Of course he wasn't lucky, and one of the assassins said, "Hey wait! Aren't you the idiot that got paid in carrots? How the hell does an idiot like you sneak past us? Hey wait a minute!"

Brandon spun, flipping the grenade he'd been holding at the assassins. The three had just enough time to yell, and the grenade went off. At least one of them went down, but Brandon didn't have time to check as laser fire began zipping by his head.

He lived on the twelfth floor of an apartment building in a dingy shit hole in an overpopulated port on the ugliest planet in the galaxy. He only lived here because it was all he could afford. The explosion from the grenade would have been heard on several floors, which meant that the cops would be coming soon. This was a problem, because most police forces were also incorporated, and would happily collect the hit on his ass to buy some new cruisers.

More assassins were bursting through his front door now, and he was finding himself surrounded. Without giving it another thought, he charged forward and dove straight through the window. The glass shattered as he slammed through it, and then he was falling. He quickly hit a button on his armor, and a small grappling hook extended from his right gauntlet. He pointed it at the adjacent building and fired. It shot through the wall with a clank, and the metal arms opened with a hiss. The strong, thin chord tightened, and he swung like a pendulum toward the building.

Suddenly a spot light was on him, and laser fire began raining down toward him. He glanced back to see the hover car closing in on him, trying to give the gunman a better shot. Brandon hit the wall hard, but managed to keep his feet moving and used the momentum from his swing to run further up the wall. Despite his heavy armor he managed to get the extra few feet he needed to clear the wall and land on the roof. He quickly retracted his grappling hook and pulled his assault rifle from his back to return fire on the hover car.

Before the hover car ascended above the roof, he caught the glint of a red laser on the side of his helmet and immediately dropped. The sniper shot went right over his head. He rolled over and saw a purple-skinned humanoid in a trench coat holding a giant sniper rifle. He immediately returned fire, and the purple thing headed for cover.

He took off running across the roof. He wasn't sure what he was going to do. The other assassins weren't even sure he was the target yet and they were still hell-bent on taking him out, apparently just to make sure.

He just needed to find a way to get to his ship. The dock was in Rego's name, so maybe they wouldn't be swarming it yet.

As the hover car rose over the roof he ducked around the side of an access door and found himself face to face with three assassins in green armor.

"Whoa, man," one of them said. "Careful coming around the corner like that, you're liable to get shot."

"Yeah," Brandon replied between breaths. "Well tell that... To our fellow assassins... That are taking shots... At me."

"What?" said another of the assassins. "That's insanity! I knew this job was gonna' get crazy! So you didn't get close to the target, did you? Have you seen him?"

"Not yet," Brandon said. "But I think I'm done with this one. Is there a way out through this building?"

"Yeah, sure pal..."

Before the assassin could finish his statement, the hover car pulled around and opened fire. Brandon had been waiting for it, and instantly dove into cover. Two of the green-armored assassins had followed suit, but the third wasn't quite quick enough and was ripped to shreds in a hail of laser fire.

The other assassins began returning fire on the hover car, and calling for back up through their communicators.

More of the black-armored assassins that had chased him out of his apartment appeared over the lip of the roof. Seeing the green-armored guys shooting at their friends in the hover car, they opened fire on the green guys. Apparently, the green guys had snipers planted on the next roof, who opened fire as well. In a matter of moments, it was an all-out war between the two teams, with Brandon caught right in the middle.

One of the green-armored guys screamed, "What the hell!? Someone is getting wrote up after this one! I guarantee it!"

Seeing how they hadn't thus far seemed interested in trying

to kill him, he decided to stick it out with the green guys for the moment, and opened fire on the black-armored guys. He managed to take down a few, and the snipers had forced the hover car to seek some measure of cover behind the building, so it was only popping up to shoot in short bursts.

Brandon took a moment to look around. All through the night sky there were hover cars, and amongst every roof top there were countless red lasers, lighting up the buildings like Christmas trees. He had never seen so many assassins working in one place, and they were all there to kill him—though he wasn't sure any of them knew which one was him. If he could just get away from the black-armored guys for a few minutes, he could blend in with the other assassins.

As he was trying to work out a plan, another of the green guys went down. The final remaining green guy grabbed the dying one, and began cursing the black-armored guys. Gun fire rained in on him, but still he held his dying comrade as he pulled a large grenade from his belt. Grenades were among his favorite things, so Brandon instantly recognized the make and model. It was powerful enough to take the whole roof apart.

The green-armored assassin made one final defiant scream and held up the grenade for all to see.

Trusting his instincts, Brandon turned and bolted for the side of the building. He jumped just as he heard the explosion behind him. The force pushed him even further out from the building. As he fell he prepared to fire his grappling hook again, but never got a chance as he landed on a hover car's windshield. The glass cracked beneath his force, and the whole car swayed violently. Both he and the assassins in the car let out a surprised yelp.

The black-armored driver instantly reached for a gun. Brandon knew there wouldn't be enough time to pull his, so instead he pointed his arm at the driver's head, quickly hitting the button for his grappling hook. With a violent thud the grappling hook shot straight through the helmeted head, and when the hooks spread there was a sound disturbingly similar to an exploding watermelon.

He quickly retracted the grappling hook, and tried to point it at the nearest building to get away. When he did this, two things occurred. The first was that the assassin in the back seat started shooting at him. The second was that when he retracted the grappling hook it yanked the driver's broken head forward and into the steering controls. The car suddenly dipped forward and started accelerating toward the ground.

The assassin in the back seemed oblivious to their impending crash, and focused solely on shooting Brandon through the broken windshield. Brandon bucked back and forth, holding on for dear life, trying to avoid being shot, and somehow trying to find a way to use his grappling hook.

"C'mon man! You're gonna' kill us both!" Brandon screamed, "Grab the damn stick!"

The assassin continued shooting at him.

"Fine! Then we both die! Dick!"

The assassin finally seemed to catch on and moved forward, pushing his buddy out of the way and taking the controls. Brandon thought it was already too late, but much to his surprise the assassin managed to level out the ship just before they hit the pavement.

"Ha!" the assassin screamed. "I did it! I can't believe it! I did it!"

"I know! Good job! You saved us both!" Brandon yelled back, then he rolled to his hip, drew his laser pistol, and shot the assassin in the head. He holstered his pistol as he jumped clear and landed on the street below.

Glancing around, he realized that there was almost as much chaos on the street as there was in the sky. It was all right, though. There might have been thousands of assassins surrounding his apartment right now, but they didn't know that Brandon Daivik was also Agkistrodon, so for the moment he could disappear. He just needed to get to his ship.

CHAPTER SIX

For a moment he thought he saw a dark form watching him from the shadows, but then chalked it up to nerves and pressed onward. He had managed to get clear of the ring of assassins around his house, and getting to the dock hadn't been too challenging after all. He and Rego had gone out of their way to make sure that they had an apartment within walking distance to their ships. Of course he hadn't counted on needing the route to save his own ass when every single idiot interested in getting rich quick was hell-bent on killing him.

It still didn't make sense. Why him? Sure he had made a few enemies here and there, every assassin did, but he couldn't think of a single one that had the kind of money to put up a million credits to have him executed. Not to mention the fact that the company shouldn't know that Brandon Daivik was Agkistrodon. But could that be it? Could it be retribution for embarrassing the company? Could this be Director Raxle Naste's way of setting an example of him? No, that didn't make sense because it was an open job. The company wouldn't even splurge to get the assassins good dental coverage; they sure as hell weren't going to spend one million credits to have his sorry ass taken out over carrots, much less invite every two-bit operation in the galaxy join in on the fun.

He was still trying to figure it out when he nearly ran right into Rego on the dock. They both gave a little jump and Brandon said, "Rego!"

Rego said, "Brandon!"

"What are you doing here?"

"I'm waiting for you! I'm glad you made it unscathed."

"So you've heard?"

"Of course. We need to hurry."

"Hurry?"

"To get you off planet, obviously. Sorry, I would have come back for you, and in fact I tried. I was here when the message about the target first came through. When I saw that it was you I thought you had rigged it to mess with me."

"I thought the same thing about you," Brandon replied with a shrug.

"Well anyway," Rego said, as he picked up a crate, "when I saw how many assassins were already moving in on the apartment I knew there was no way that I could get to you in time. So I came here to wait. You seem to have gotten away clean."

"Clean!?" Brandon shrieked.

"Hey, you're here in one piece."

"I jumped out the window of our apartment and used my grappling hook to swing to the next building over..."

"Okay."

"I started a war between two different assassin teams and a bunch of people got killed."

"Alright."

"I rode the windshield of a crashing hover car..."

"I get it," Rego said. "A lot of stuff happened. Now hurry up. I've already got my ship prepped to get you off planet."

Brandon stared at his roommate for a moment. Did he trust Rego? He had known him for a few years, and had said before that he would trust him with his life. Now, with his life actually on the line, he wasn't quite so sure. If he couldn't trust Rego, who could he trust? He knew he couldn't do it on his own, so he was more or less forced to trust Rego.

"Alright, Rego. Where are we headed?"

"It's a secret," Rego said. "Or rather a secret compound that my team uses occasionally."

Brandon nodded. A lot of assassins chose to work in teams. Brandon had temporarily formed alliances with other assassins and teams before, but he had never actually become a full-time member of one. Rego on the other hand was. He was part of team Senrath, a fairly large and successful group of assassins. If Brandon was remembering right, there were close to thirty members.

It wasn't easy to get on to a team full time, but there were definitely some perks. For example they split the pay, so even when some of the members weren't involved in a hit, they still made money. Being on a team meant always having someone to watch your back. Some of the more successful teams even hired their own weapons and armor repairmen. Big teams like Senrath even had their own secret bases hidden throughout the galaxy.

Brandon glanced at Rego and nodded. "Okay, hidden base sounds good, but I'm not sure. I mean, no offense, but I hardly trust you—your teammates don't even know me. They have no reason to be loyal to me. I'm sure they would be happy to execute me and collect the money."

Rego nodded. "That's why you are going to make sure you stay in your armor. The dossier didn't mention anything about Brandon the assassin, just Brandon Daivik the human. As long as you keep your face covered up no one will know the difference until the company realizes that the person they're after works for them."

"Yeah, well I can't imagine that will take long."

"Probably not," Rego said. "But we are just going to hit the base long enough to resupply and see if we can figure out what's going on, then we'll get out of there. Besides, the whole team will probably be away from the base hunting you anyway, and I doubt anyone will realize the connection for a day or two. Hell, they might not realize it at all, Mr. Mecrevice."

"Now there's a happy thought," Brandon replied. "Alright let's do it your way. We taking your ship or mine?"

"Mine of course," Rego said. "It's faster and better looking than yours."

"So you have no idea who put this hit on you?" Rego asked.

Brandon lay back in the bucket seat and kicked his feet up. They were only a few minutes out from their destination, and trepidation tore through his nervous system like a laser bolt. He was as safe as he could be for the moment, traveling through hyperspace, but still he couldn't shake the feeling that his days, or minutes, were numbered. Anywhere he went now someone would be hunting him. Someone would be trying to kill him.

He shrugged at his friend. "I haven't the slightest idea. Even if someone in the company knows who I am, surely they aren't this pissed over the carrots."

Rego rubbed his green chin thoughtfully and said, "Okay, well who have you pissed off recently that has a lot of money?"

"Well, I might have pissed off the people that Rharo Staris owed money to. And I might have pissed off the casino, too," Brandon admitted. "But I just can't see any of them putting up this many credits for my sorry ass."

"Anyone else you've pissed off with the kind of money to put this big of a hit on you?"

Brandon threw up his hands defensively. "Assassins Incorporated."

Rego shook his head. "Nah, the company wouldn't spend that kind of money to kill one of its own. If the company wanted you dead, then you would have woke up to Naja Ashei standing over your dying body."

"Another happy thought. Thanks, buddy."

Rego shrugged. "All I'm saying is that when Naja Ashei comes after you... And you know that he will... I no longer have your back. When Naja Ashei comes for you, you are on your own."

"Thanks man," Brandon said. "I appreciate that."

Rego laughed. "He's the best. And my money is on him being the first one to find you. You may never become the greatest assassin in the galaxy, but you may get to be killed by the greatest assassin in the galaxy."

Brandon didn't even bother to reply.

Rego continued. "Well I do know one thing for sure."

"What's that?"

"That you won't be the one claiming the prize for this hit and clearing your name like you had hoped."

"No shit."

CHAPTER SEVEN

"A trash world," Brandon said. "What a great place for a secret hideout."

He watched in wonder as the nearby crane arm moved a pile of trash as big as the ship. There were various pieces of robotic equipment all around that he didn't quite understand. It appeared some were melting and burning trash while others were trying to condense it. And the trash! He had never seen so much trash in his life. Mountain-sized piles of trash stabbed into the dull, brown sky. He glanced back at Rego. "I always kind of wondered about trash planets, but I guess they are exactly what they sound like."

"Yeah," Rego said. "With all of the new galactic sanitation laws, trash planets are becoming more popular. Thousands of giant ships pour in here each day from hundreds of different planets to drop off more trash."

"Seems like an expensive way to get rid of garbage."

"You'd think," Rego said. "But robots sort the trash, and some of the burn off is used to fuel the giant ships, so other than the initial cost of the ship and repairs, there's no real expense. They choose a planet void of sentient life and dump away. Why worry about the eco-system of a planet with no life?"

Brandon nodded. "You sure know a lot about trash planets."

Rego laughed. "Well like I said, my secret base is here. Which reminds me, if you end up outside make sure that you have your suit environmental protectors on. You can't breathe the air."

"No kidding," Brandon said, taking in the brown sky again. "What's the name of this planet?"

Rego smiled. "I can't tell you. It's bad enough that I'm bringing a guest to the hideout. If my team found out that I told someone the planet it was on I would get booted for sure.

"Fine. Just curious."

"Well, watch this."

Rego lowered the ship down beside a mountain of trash. As they descended further, Brandon noticed a giant cave cut into the side of the mountain.

As Rego maneuvered the ship into the giant cave he said, "And this is the entrance to our base."

A little way ahead of them a giant blast door began to open. Rego carefully maneuvered the ship in.

"You've got to be kidding me," Brandon said. "I can't believe you never told me about this!"

Rego shrugged. "Look, just like I said. It doesn't appear that anyone's home."

Brandon glanced out and realized that he was looking at an empty ship bay, and felt a little bit better about the situation.

As the ship gently landed Rego said, "Now, let's go see what my teammates left to eat."

"Wow, this place is huge," Brandon said. "It's like a giant bunker. I don't think I'd be able to find my way back out of here. What was this place for originally?"

"I'm not sure," Rego said. "I think maybe as a maintenance facility for repairing trash equipment. That's just a guess though."

Brandon nodded and looked around again. They were in a long hallway with a concrete floor, walls, and ceiling. Small lights cast a blue ambience that lighted their way. They had already passed through several secure doors and switched directions in the hallways enough that Brandon had completely lost any sense of direction. If Rego's teammates decided to show up and take him out, he would be trapped. He tried not to think about it and focused on following Rego.

The next room they entered was fairly large and had various equipment crates stacked around. It looked like a disorganized storage room. Brandon asked, "What's this place, Rego?"

"Storage."

"Thanks, buddy. Very informative tour. Are we at least close to where we're heading?"

"Very."

Brandon sighed in frustration and growled, "You aren't very..."

He was cut off by blinding light, the sound of shuffling feet, and weapons being drawn. Before the light cleared and his vision returned, he already knew what was happening. He had been betrayed. He shook his head and said, "Dammit, Rego."

The blinding lights were pulled away, and he found himself surrounded by approximately thirty assassins in blue and black armor matching Rego's. Most were wearing their helmets and had their faces covered. All were armed, and all arms were pointing at him.

Rego turned around and with a sincere face said, "Sorry

buddy."

"Really? You're sorry? Really?"

Rego ignored him and turned to a rather large armored figure standing in the center, and giving a nod said, "Commander."

The figure stepped forward, and with a husky alien voice said, "So this is our man, huh? Doesn't look like much. Any idea why there's such a lofty price on his head?"

Rego shook his head. "No clue, boss. He doesn't know, either. It's a mystery."

"Shame," said the Commander. "A man ought to at least know who's killing him before he dies. Ah, well. You still want to do this your way, Rego? Or would you prefer we just blast him?"

"We'll do it my way still if it's all the same to you. He is my best friend after all."

The Commander nodded. "Fair enough, though I think we may have over done it a bit."

Rego shook his head and glanced back at Brandon. "No, best to play it safe with this one. Don't let him fool you, he is resourceful under pressure... Or at least he knows how to make a mess of things. When the other assassins first approached him at the apartment he managed to get two factions facing off against one another, with fatalities."

"Wow," the Commander said. "That's almost unheard of this day and age. HR's gonna have a field day with all of the write ups."

"Don't forget the part where I rode the crashing hover car's windshield. That's the best part. Or how I shot that guy in the head with my grappling hook, except he was the driver, and that was kind of the reason the hover car was starting to crash. But then, I managed to talk the assassin in the back seat into not shooting at me so he could land the car safely. And then he actually managed to land it, so I shot him in the head."

"Does he always ramble like this?" the Commander asked.

"Unfortunately," Rego confirmed.

"That's not true! I'm assuming I've only got a few minutes to live, so I might as well air out a few of my accomplishments. Like, for example, one time I got paid in carrots for killing a guy in the middle of a casino."

"You're the carrots guy?" the Commander asked. "We've all heard about that."

"Of course you have."

Chuckles went up from the armed assassins surrounding

him.

"You're pretty much like a celebrity," the Commander said. "Did you know the casino floor manager got fired?

"Hmm," Brandon said. "That's disappointing."

"Not exactly an accomplishment," Rego said. "Maybe stick to the good things, buddy."

"First off, the moment you betrayed me we stopped being buddies. Second thing, it's all about how you look at it. A lot of people have laughed about the carrot situation, which means that I've brought joy to people's hearts. Which in my opinion, makes it an accomplishment. And what accomplishment do you have to brag about, Rego? Oh you stabbed your best friend in the back and got him killed for money!"

"It's not personal, Brandon," Rego said. "It's just business. You are months behind on the bills. I didn't want to lose the apartment and be kicked out on the street. Surely, you can understand. I mean... You would have done the same thing."

"Are you serious!? You sold me out because I'm behind on the bills! That is just.... You are the shittiest friend ever! And no! I most certainly wouldn't have done that to you!!!" Brandon screamed. "Oh and I've told you, when I'm in the armor, it's Agkistromotherfuckingdon!!! You dick!"

"I wouldn't be too hard on your friend," the Commander said. "He could have just gunned you down, you know."

"Yeah, you're right," Brandon said. "Why go through all of this shit? Why not just shoot me in the back?"

"I have to let my team in on the cut either way, so I figured I might as well utilize them," Rego said with a shrug. "Besides, this way there is no question who killed you."

The Commander continued. "No reason to hold back the whole truth, Rego. The man is about to die. He should at least know."

Rego nodded. "And because I didn't want you to suffer. I knew that if I tried to take you out myself somehow you would screw it up and I would have to hurt you. Will one of you guys start taking his guns and grenades? Especially the grenades; he's actually pretty good with the damn things. He likes to set the charges for only a second or two. Amazing he hasn't killed himself yet... Anyway, I figured if we took your weapons away you couldn't really fight, and I could give you a shot of Loxer-Bloov, which will basically make you go to sleep and never wake up. No pain."

"That's actually... That's actually kind of sweet," Brandon said.

"But you're still the shittiest friend ever, and I'm quick on the draw, too. Don't forget that."

Rego sighed and shook his head.

Brandon didn't fight while they took his guns, and it actually took more than one guy to hold all of them. Three to be exact. When he found out that most of the galaxy was out to kill him he had dressed for the occasion. Not that it mattered now. He sighed and said, "Can we get on with this? I don't have all day."

Rego nodded. "I believe we are ready to move forward with this. From this point, if you try to resist in any way my team will gun you down."

The Commander turned to Rego. "How many do you want to finish this thing?"

"Six should be enough," Rego said.

"Six ain't enough to stop me," Brandon spat. "Better make it eight."

They paused and stared at him for a moment, and then Rego said, "Maybe eight just in case he tries something."

The Commander nodded and selected eight assassins. Four got behind Brandon. Four got in front of him and turned to face him.

"Alright," Rego said. "We're going someplace more private so you can retain some dignity, my friend."

"Dignity? Really?" Brandon said. "The guy that just sold out his best friend wants to talk about dignity."

"Let's go," Rego said, and began marching forward. Brandon and his eight escorts, with all of their guns pointed at his chest, followed.

CHAPTER EIGHT

Rego led them down another hallway, and again Brandon was lost in the maze of this facility. A part of him wanted to try to make a move, but he knew realistically there was no way that he would succeed. Even if he managed to take out one or two of them he would still be gunned down. What good would that do? With the exception of Rego, who was a back-stabbing dick, the others were just doing their job. They were doing the same job that he'd loved so much. He could hardly blame them for that. And on top of that, he didn't really want to get scorched to death with lasers. If one had to be executed, Rego's execution didn't sound half bad.

"If you have any last wishes or final statements," Rego said, glancing over his shoulder, "now would be the time, Brandon."

"Agkistrodon," Brandon replied.

"Right," Rego sighed, but stopped bothering to glance back. "If you have any final wishes, I would do my best to fulfill them for you."

"Would you? Really? Would...." Brandon paused. "Actually there is one thing. My mom has been calling and leaving me messages for the past few days. Would you mind if I called her real quick?"

"You never want to call your mom," Rego said, and a hint of suspicion spread across his green face.

"Yeah," Brandon said, "but it's not every day that I'm about to die, now is it? I'll feel like shit if I don't at least call her back real quick. I'll keep it short."

"I've seen you on the phone with your mother. There is no such thing as keeping it short."

"Yeah, well this time I will. Are you really going to deny me the right to call my mom?"

Rego sighed. "Fine, but make it quick!"

"I don't guess that I can do this in privacy?"

Rego glared at him, and the others didn't say anything. Brandon shrugged and said, "Alright but you guys have got to keep quiet. My mother has no idea that I'm an assassin. She thinks I'm in telemarketing."

"Seriously?" asked one of the soldiers.

"Yes, he's serious," Rego said.

"Alright guys, shhhh," Brandon said, as he dialed his mom up on his communicator. He could have turned it to in-helmet only, but he figured the least he could do was make the assassins suffer through the phone call with him.

After the first four rings, he growled, "Seriously? She's been calling me for days!"

After the fifth ring, "Really!? Really, Mom!? About to die here!"

After the sixth ring it rolled over to messaging, and he ended the call stating, "Well I'm certainly not going to leave her a message. That's just cryptic."

"Can we continue onward now?" Rego asked.

"Yup," Brandon said, "nothing left but to die now I guess."

A few more hallways, secured metal doors, and about five minutes later Brandon found himself standing in another storage room, but this one seemed a little more vacated and everything was covered in dust. As if reading his mind Rego said, "I'm told this storage room hasn't been used for much in the past ten years or so. It seemed like a more appropriate place. I'll prepare the medicine. Once you've had your shot, we'll lock you in here so that you can die in privacy."

"Wow, Rego. How very thoughtful of you. Dick!"

"I was really hoping that you would be more understanding, Brandon," Rego said. "We've always been such good friends. I was really hoping that you wouldn't think of me as an enemy."

"Rego, you are killing me for money. That's pretty much the definition of enemy, you idiot. We aren't friends anymore."

Rego shook his head and turned around to begin fiddling with his needle. Brandon didn't know what exactly went into preparing the needle, but he couldn't imagine that it would take long. As far as he could tell, he was moments away from the end.

He glanced around at his guards for any sign of a weak point and found none. All eight were facing him, assault rifles pointed at his face. There was literally nothing he could do without a distraction of some sort.

There was a sudden flicker of light, and in a moment he realized that he had missed his only opportunity as all of the guard's looked up briefly. By the time he realized the opportunity had presented itself it was already too late, and the guards were looking at him again.

"That was weird," one of the guards said. "We never have power issues in this base."

The lights flicked out again, and when they reappeared, he thought he saw a dark from beside Rego. Then the lights were out again, and Brandon heard a swooshing sound followed by a thump. When the lights came back on, the dark form was gone, and only Rego and the guards remained. Brandon was still trying to figure out if his mind was playing tricks on him as he watched in slow motion as Rego's head slid away from his body and fell to the floor.

"Holy shit!" Brandon bellowed.

The guards were all so focused on him, that none of them seemed to notice the headless body of Rego falling to the floor, much less the dark form dropping from the ceiling. Brandon saw the attack coming and instantly ducked. The dark form landed right in the middle of the guards, and before anyone could react, two more headless bodies dropped to the floor. Continuing through with his momentum, the figure hurled three small objects that looked like ninja stars, but apparently were wrapped in some kind of chain blade tech, that tore right through armor. Three more of the guards went down. The next tried to bring his assault rifle to bear on the dark form, but his sword slapped it away and he stepped in slamming a knife into the guard's throat. The final guard turned to run, but the attacker dove over him and spun, driving his sword through the guard's chest.

As this was happening, Brandon took the moment to scoop up a fallen laser rifle and turned just in time to find himself facing the glowing white 'X' shaped eyes of Naja Ashei, the best assassin in the business.

Naja Ashei stared at him silently, holding his sword at his side. Brandon stared back, and after a few very long moments asked, "Are you here to kill me?"

Naja Ashei cocked his head ever so slightly and said, "What would make you think that I want to kill you?"

"The last time I saw you, you shot me."

Naja shrugged. "Shot... Didn't kill. If I had wanted you dead, I would have killed you."

"I spent three days in the hospital," Brandon replied.

Naja shrugged again and said, "I had to make sure that you knew going after my targets was a no no."

"So you aren't here to collect the big money for killing me?"

"Of course not, don't be so petty," Naja said. "Why haven't you been returning mom's messages? She's practically going nuts."

"More of a reason not to call her."

"That's not fair to Dad and me. When you don't talk to her we have to deal with the fallout."

"Oh, like I didn't have to deal with the fallout when you left home to become an assassin. She went insane. I still don't think she's recovered from it."

"I was just trying to follow in Dad's footsteps."

"Yeah," Brandon said. "And so am I. I was just smart enough to come up with a good lie for mom."

"Right," Naja replied, "because you're a telemarketer, not a cut-rate assassin who takes carrots as payment."

"Oh really? Is that why you came to rescue me? So you could rib me about the damn carrots?"

Naja shrugged. "Everyone knows that Feeintan Quarris has a carrot-based economy."

"I absolutely did not know that!" Brandon spat. "But I might have, if my big brother would have gone out of his way to show me the ropes in this business, instead of... I don't know... Shooting me!"

"Oh don't you try to blame this on me. Dad told me that if I wanted to get into this business I had to learn myself. I've only treated you the exact same way."

"Really? So Dad shot you?"

"Well, no, but that was different."

"How?"

"You were going after my target," Naja said. "Plus I owed you one for stealing my name idea."

"Your name idea!?"

"Yeah, Naja Ashei is the scientific name for a cobra snake back on Earth. Then you come rolling out with Agkistrodon."

"No dick, I know what Naja Ashei means, but you stole the idea from me!"

"How do you figure?"

"When I was seven and you were twelve, we got to see Dad in his armor for the first time. I distinctly remember saying that when I grew up I was going to be an assassin just like Dad, and that I was going to use a cool snake name. And you told me it was a stupid idea."

"I don't remember that," Naja said. "And we both stole the idea from Dad anyway."

"Yeah, but Dad used a mammal name! You stole the snake

idea from me!"

"Yes, but Agkistrodon is a stupid name anyway. You sound like a dinosaur."

"And Naja Ashei makes it sound like you are a belly dancer!"

"You act like I didn't help you at all!" Naja yelled. "I helped you acquire a false identity, didn't I?"

"Oh, yeah, Philup Mecrevice! What a brilliant, fucking name! Thank you so much, big brother!" Brandon screamed back. "And a lot of fucking good it's doing me with half the galaxy after my ass!"

Naja chuckled and shook his head. "There's just no talking to you. Much too stubborn. You haven't even thanked me for saving your life yet."

"We aren't off this trash heap yet... But thank you, big brother," Brandon spat through gritted teeth. "Now can we get the hell out of here?"

"As soon as you promise that you will call Mom."

"I actually just did a few minutes ago, and she didn't answer."

"Wait," Naja said. "You called her a few minutes ago? From your personal communicator account?"

"Well yeah, I wasn't going to call her from my Agkistrodon account. She doesn't know I'm an assassin, remember?"

"How long ago did you call!?"

Brandon shrugged, confused by his brother's sudden excitement. "I don't know... Like maybe ten minutes now."

"Damn! We've got to hurry!"

"What? Why?"

"You just made a communication call as Brandon Daivik. You better believe your account has been traced. Half the galaxy is probably headed here right now. This place is going to be swarming with assassins in a few minutes."

"Son of a..."

"C'mon," Naja cut him off. "We've got to go."

CHAPTER NINE

"You know the way out?" Brandon asked.

"Of course."

Brandon struggled for breath as he tried to keep up with the lithe form of his brother. He kept telling himself it was because Naja wore much lighter armor, but he knew it was really because his brother went through rigorous daily workouts. The galaxy's number-one assassin trained his body to be a weapon. His very being was the perfected assassin's tool. Brandon on the other hand, not so much. He always told himself he was going to get motivated to lose that little bit of extra fluff around his waist, but he really never got around to it.

The long hallways were just as confusing going out as they had been coming in. In fact, he wasn't completely sure that they were even going back the same way. They might have been in a whole new section of the hidden base for all he knew.

Naja paused at the next intersection, and Brandon leaned over to catch his breath. After a moment he noticed that his brother was staring at him and shaking his head. Brandon coughed and rasped out, "Shut up."

"Silence," Naja whispered back. "I'm trying to listen over the sound of your breathing. We may have trouble up ahead."

Brandon attempted to control his breathing and made sure that the safety was off on his stolen rifle. If they ran into trouble, he would rather have had his own gear, but that wasn't an option. The rifle he had commandeered from the dead guard would have to do.

Naja leaned in closer and whispered, "There are enemies in a room around the corner. Not sure how many. I don't think we will be able to sneak around them. Your breathing is too loud and you stomp like a vulbisarious in heat."

Brandon stuck his tongue out, but put it back in his mouth when his exhausted mind realized that he was still wearing his helmet. His brother, whose real name was Jack, had always been an asshole. Even when they were growing up he had always sought to belittle and demean Brandon. They had grown up in a small rural area that was years behind on technology. While other kids their age were playing Graphic Challenge Simulators, they grew up running through the forest and living like their forefathers. This may have been why Jack had grown up to be so athletic. Jack had also been good with the girls. Brandon on the other hand, had just never really found his niche.

His brother had always made sure to let him know that he was useless as often as possible. Some people had said that Brandon was smart because he had good grades in school, but the truth was he had to work at it. Jack only tried in school when he absolutely had to, but when he decided to try at something he always excelled regardless of what it was. The only thing that Brandon thought his brother had failed at was humility.

"Brandon," Jack hissed.

Brandon snapped back to reality and glanced up at his brother. "Sorry."

Jack shook his head and said, "We are going to have to strike quickly. Stay behind me, and shoot anyone that I miss. Got it?"

Brandon nodded, and without another word Jack headed around the corner. Brandon followed and a moment later they approached the room with the enemies inside. He couldn't tell for sure how many there were. At least four or five.

Before Brandon even knew what was going on, his brother was in the room and on the attack. He moved with uncanny speed and grace. The enemy saw him and attempted to react, but by the time they tried he was already moving again. There had been six of them in all. The one sitting closest to the door he had decapitated on the way through. Then he had spun and his hand had flailed out two of the ninja star things which had planted firmly in the necks of two men across the room. By this point the guards still weren't sure what was going on. As he rolled forward and disemboweled the next man, the remaining two finally came to life and started reaching for guns. However by the time that their guns were in their hands, Naja Ashei was upon them. The first he reached took a sword blade through the throat. The final man he finished in the way he had started, with a swift decapitation.

When the killing was finished, Brandon strolled calmly into the room. It was a small break room slash storage area. As Jack wiped the blood from his sword, the cold, masked face of Naja Ashei turned to face him. "Thanks for all of the help."

Brandon shrugged. "You seemed to have it under control."

Jack shook his head and said, "Probably for the best. You

would have made too much noise with your gun. At least this way they still don't know that we're on the move yet."

"Hey look at that," Brandon said. "This is where they put my gear."

Approaching a small table he found his arsenal laid out before him. He quickly began reattaching guns, knives, grenades, and other useful trinkets back to their rightful places on his armor. It was something of a process, and Jack kept nagging about needing to hurry. As he continued strapping on his gear he said, "They must have another ship bay, because the one that we came in didn't have any ships in it."

"They do, but it's less of a bay and more of a ship yard. Your friend Rego brought you in through the back door to make you think that no one else was here. He wanted you to feel comfortable. They actually have a much larger front door and park their ships outside. You didn't find it strange that on a trash planet they would need to hide the entrance to their base? Who's going to come looking for it?"

Brandon nodded. "Makes sense, but where's your ship?"

"It's not here."

"Not here?" Brandon asked. "Then how did you get here?"

"I rode on Rego's ship with you."

He could just picture the cocky smile beneath the black armored face. He wanted to slap his brother, but instead said, "Then why didn't you rescue me before we got here?"

"Because I didn't know that your friend was going to betray you until we got here. His plan had some merit, so I decided to wait things out until I knew for sure that he intended to betray you."

"Okay, so where's your ship? How are we getting off of this trash heap?"

"We have a ride coming to pick us up. We just have to sneak out the front door. Of course, I hadn't planned on you making a call from your personal account, so that might make it a bit trickier. Hopefully our ride will get here in time."

"Who's coming to pick us up?"

Jack ignored him and said, "Hurry up. We need to sneak out the front door before half of the galaxy gets here to kill you."

CHAPTER TEN

Jack killed the two Senrath guys watching the front door with ease and brutality. It was a gruesome display, and when he was done there was an excessive amount of blood and parts everywhere.

"You call this sneaking?" Brandon asked.

Jack ignored him and said, "C'mon."

Brandon shook his head and followed his brother. They were standing in a small office beside two large double doors which he could only assume were the front doors to the facility. If there were members of Rego's Senrath team outside, they would see them the moment they walked through the giant doors. Fortunately, it appeared that Jack knew another way out and was leading them through a small hallway out the back of the office.

"How the hell do you know this base so well?" Brandon asked.

"I make a point of knowing the layouts of as many hideouts as I can. You never know when you might need to get your kill right out from under your opponent's nose. Which I actually did once to team Senrath. Their commander is still butt hurt about that, mostly because they don't know how I did it."

"Show off," Brandon said, but he couldn't help but to feel just a little better about his brother being the best assassin in the galaxy, at least for a moment.

They approached a small utility door, but before Jack opened it he said, "This leads outside. As soon as we open this we will be out in the open. Last time I was here they had a lot of old steel crates and stuff stacked outside. If they are still there it could provide us a decent amount of cover, however there is no guarantee that they are still there. This ship yard is fairly large, and can hold twenty or so small ships like Rego's. It's circular, and surrounded by large mounds of trash. Got it?"

Brandon nodded.

"Do you have your suit environmental protections on? The air outside of the facility isn't safe."

"Yeah, Rego mentioned that," Brandon said, even though he had forgotten until Jack reminded him.

As he turned the protections on, his brother shook his head

and then pulled a small metal square from his back. He pressed a button and it unfolded and transformed into a full-sized assault rifle. He continued, "As soon as we step out we may be seen. If that's the case, we open fire and haul ass to the closest available cover. If there isn't any cover we retreat back inside. Got it?"

Brandon nodded and made sure that his own assault rifle was ready. He was rather glad to have his own rifle back. It wasn't anything particularly special. It certainly wasn't retractable like his brother's and probably only cost a fraction of the price. However, it was his rifle and he was much more comfortable going into a combat situation carrying it.

Jack stared back at him, patiently waiting for him to get ready. Brandon popped his neck and gave his brother a nod. Jack opened the door.

They stepped outside, and for a moment the light of the brown sky hurt his eyes after being inside the dark building, but his helmet quickly adjusted for brightness. Thirty or forty yards across from them were several ships, and standing around them were the remaining members of team Senrath. Jack had opened the door quietly enough that they weren't immediately noticed.

He picked out the commander restlessly moving around and heard him say, "Rego needs to hurry up. I know killing his friend is tough, but we need to get it done and get paid."

"I couldn't agree more boss," another blue-armored individual said.

"Someone needs to call him," the commander added as he kicked the dirt and turned his head towards Brandon. "This is taking way too..." Before he had time to finish his statement both Brandon and Jack were hurling grenades at him.

"Move!" the commander screamed and dove for cover.

The grenades exploded a moment later, buying the brothers a few precious seconds. Jack turned and ran straight towards some large metal containers to their left. Brandon followed suit, and dove into cover just as their attackers began opening fire.

Jack pulled out a small device and held it over the top of the crate. It only took Brandon a moment to realize that it was a camera that was probably tied directly into his brother's helmet.

Jack said, "At least four are down."

"Ha," Brandon said. "Well at least we are alike in some ways. Dad would be proud to have seen us both hurl grenades at the same time like that!"

"Don't get too excited," Jack said. "Mine took out the four

guys. Yours missed completely."

"Oh bull shit," Brandon said. "Don't be stingy."

"I'm serious."

"Whatever, let's see who gets more kills while we wait for this ride of yours."

The glowing white X's turned toward him for a moment, and Jack said, "Are you sure you want to compete for kills with the number one assassin in the galaxy?"

"You're such a dick," Brandon said, as he leaned around the crate and began returning fire. He dropped two men that were still in the open, and was about to make a comment to his brother when Jack leaned over the top and cleanly picked off three with his own rifle. Again he could just picture the shit-eating grin on his brother's face.

The shouts from the Senrath guys were starting to get more organized, and the fact that his brother was the most feared assassin in the galaxy didn't change the fact that they were outnumbered. If the Senrath crew got organized, they were screwed.

Brandon leaned out and fired a few more pop shots, but didn't hit anything before he had to pull back into cover. Jack leaned over the top and fired a few more shots as well, but Brandon had no way of knowing if he hit anything.

One of the Senrath guys yelled, "Is that Naja Ashei!?"

Another screamed, "It can't be! He wouldn't be helping the mark!"

The commander's voice drowned out the others, screaming, "All men outside! The mark is outside! Rego where are you at!?"

"Rego ain't coming!" Brandon yelled from cover.

"He's dead?" the commander asked, and the gun fire came to a halt for a moment.

"Yup," Brandon replied.

"You killed him? After the mercy that he was showing you?"

"Mercy my ass!" Brandon said. "But I didn't kill him. Naja Ashei did. You'll find his body in the storage room, but the head might have rolled away. Naja is brutal like that. I would suggest you fellas' back off so you don't end up like the rest of your comrades inside."

Brandon turned and shrugged at his brother, and in a low voice said, "It's worth a shot."

Jack shrugged back.

The commander yelled, "Is that really you Naja Ashei?"

Jack laughed and said, "Why don't you come over here and

find out Commander Veekan?"

The commander, whose name was apparently Veekan, yelled, "We still owe you one for the Trigante ordeal!"

Brandon leaned closer to his brother and said, "Just making friends everywhere you go, eh?"

"This coming from the guy with galaxy's biggest price on his head," Jack responded.

Another Senrath guy said, "Commander I don't know if taking on Naja Ashei is..."

"Be silent!" Commander Veekan rasped. "There's only two of them, and one of them is a complete idiot."

Jack leaned closer to Brandon and said, "Wonder which one of us that could be?"

"What a dick," Brandon growled. Then he leaned out and hurled a grenade at where he thought Commander Veekan's voice was coming from. It exploded a moment later, and while Brandon wasn't sure what he hit, the gun fire started up immediately, and he heard Commander Veekan giving orders.

Jack used his small camera again and said, "They are trying to flank us to the right. Get a grenade out there."

"Okay, but I've only got three more," Brandon said as he leaned out and hurled a grenade to the right. He had just enough time to see this one land in between three guys trying to creep around before he had to duck back into cover. A moment later the grenade exploded, and he smiled with satisfaction as he heard three screams.

Brandon laughed and said, "Did you see that?"

Jack ignored him and said, "Look up."

Brandon did and saw the ships appearing through the atmosphere. At first he could only see three, but as they drew closer he saw another five or six behind them. Apparently, his brother had been right about the other assassins tracking his call from his personal account. "Son of a bitch!"

CHAPTER ELEVEN

As he watched the ships moving in, he leaned toward Jack. "Well, maybe they haven't made the Agkistrodon connection yet."

As he was making this statement the first of the ships swooped in from above them. It was a mid-sized ship, typical of most assassins. Brandon's was a smaller old clunker, but he was poor. Jack had a sleek ship, a custom job that was faster and had better shielding than most of the ships out there. However, the one moving in above them was a fairly typical model.

There was a clinking sound and a door opened on the bottom side of the ship. Three red-clad assassins descended from long cords, and immediately began firing at them.

As they ducked lower into cover Jack said, "Apparently they've figured it out."

"Well that didn't take long," Brandon grumbled. "Can't they see it's you? What good is being the best assassin in the galaxy if no one is scared of you?"

Jack didn't bother with an immediate reply, but instead pulled a long, cylindrical object from behind his back. He held it up to the front of his rifle and pressed a button. The cylinder attached to the barrel and then extended out, making his barrel significantly longer. He then applied another small metal piece to the top, which unfolded into a scope. Before Brandon could mention how impressed he was, Jack said, "I'll cover the sky, you keep the pressure on the ground forces."

Without another reply, Jack leaned out and carefully picked off all three of the red-armored men. They were left dangling by their cords, and the ship decided it was wise to back off. As soon as it did another moved in, and a two figures in purple armor dove out. They had hover tech on their suits and began gracefully swooping toward them, all while firing their weapons. Jack, shot them both out of the sky.

Brandon stifled his amazement and focused on his assignment. He leaned out from the side and took a few pop shots at the Senrath guys again, but didn't hit anything. In the moment he stuck his head out he could see that many of the ships were landing, and ground forces were beginning to pour out. A moment later, when he took the next shot, he could see that the additional ground forces were moving closer.

He rolled back toward Jack and said, "Do you recognize any of the ships out there?"

Jack shot an orange-armored assassin diving toward them with a jetpack. The body held its course and smashed into the trash pile behind them, then rolled a few times and was lost in a trashalanch.

Jack turned to his brother and said, "About half of them are with Assassins Inc., a few others are Bounty Hunters Association, and the others are probably random mercs. Why?"

"Because," Brandon said as he leaned out to shoot again, "it would certainly be nice if we could get them to start killing each other before they completely overrun us."

"That's the smartest thing you've ever said," Jack replied, and pressed a button on his wrist. A moment later he said, "Barista. Is that your ship I see out there?"

A rather baritone alien voice responded, "Yeah Naja. Where are you at? I don't see you or your ship."

"Of course not," Jack replied.

Barista's laugh was a gasping hollow sound. "Of course not. So what can I do for you?"

Brandon had been working on trying to sound intimidating when he was on the job. Assassins Inc. even offered classes, but he didn't think he could ever match the icy tone that his brother used when he was Naja Ashei. He had seen his brother in action, but that voice sent icy chills down his spine.

Jack said, "Vice President Lynx Rufus clearly stated that he wanted Kazor Sect to get this hit. I see ships in the sky that aren't part of Assassins Inc. It would be embarrassing to the company if one of those guys gets the hit. There's enough gun fire aimed at the target right now to make that a possibility. That needs to change immediately."

"What are you saying?" Barista asked.

"Anyone that isn't a member of Assassins Incorporated is fair game," Jack said. "Burn the ground and wipe their ships out of the sky."

The silence lingered for a moment, and Brandon didn't think there was going to be a response. Finally Barista said, "Alright. Whatever you say, Naja Ashei."

A moment later, a large black warship swiveled around and began firing on a smaller ship. Brandon assumed this much bigger one must be Barista's ship. The smaller ship was ill equipped and completely unprepared for the assault. It was a falling pile of ash before it ever hit the ground.

The giant warship immediately went to work on another ship, and several other ships began picking targets as well. Barista had apparently spread the word around to the other Assassins Inc. vessels. Most assassins would have been hesitant to open fire on the other ships, as this was not a typically accepted practice in the corporate killing business, but when an order came down from someone like Naja Ashei, heads rolled. Literally.

Brandon was able to quickly tell the forces apart. The Bounty Hunter Association ships were the ones trying to get away, because they knew what they were up against. The random merc ships were the ones mostly trying to fight back, unaware that it had become a group effort. The Assassins Incorporated ships were of course the ones wreaking havoc on everyone else.

Brandon peaked around and saw that the story on the ground wasn't much different. There had to be at least one hundred ground fighters, and they were killing each other now, too.

Brandon laughed. "I can't believe that actually worked!"

He had just enough time to finish this statement and then something smashed into him. His body smacked against the ground, and would have been broken if it wasn't for his armor. Still as he rolled to his knees his vision was swimming and he staggered as he tried to rise. Looking up he realized what had hit him was in fact the very steel canister that they had been hiding behind. There was smoke rising over the top of the crate, and he thought that it may have been hit by a rocket. He glanced over and saw that his brother was several paces away, lying on the ground and not moving.

He heard the hydraulic hiss of a door opening, and glanced back toward the canisters. As the smoke cleared he saw Commander Veekan step out of what appeared to be some kind of hover tractor, presumably for moving the heavy steel canisters. He had apparently crashed into the canisters as hard as he could, and Brandon had to admit it had been rather effective.

Commander Veekan hit the ground and drew a long-bladed knife. He pressed a button, and the blade turned bright red. Brandon knew that it would cut right through his armor. He staggered to rise again and fell back to his knees. He was helpless, and there was nothing he could do to stop Commander Veekan from killing him.

Much to his surprise, Commander Veekan turned toward Jack instead. As he stomped toward him he said, "I told you one day I would have my revenge, Naja! Today I'll be remembered as the assassin that took out Naja Ashei!"

Jack still wasn't moving, and Brandon had no doubt Commander Veekan would kill his brother. He gritted his teeth, dug down deep, and let out a snarl as he charged back to his feet. He was still disoriented, but his feet obeyed his commands. He sprinted forward with everything he had and speared Commander Veekan from behind.

He wasn't sure what species Commander Veekan was, but it was like hitting a brick wall. Still, the unsuspecting Commander was slammed against a crate, and Brandon fell beside him. Commander Veekan let loose his own snarl and spun on Brandon. The laser knife came down toward his helmet, but Brandon managed to slap it away just before it struck, and sent the blade skimming across the top of his helmet with a violent hiss.

Commander Veekan kicked out, planting a boot right into Brandon's chest plate and knocked him back to the ground. He tried to rise, but wasn't quite quick enough as Commander Veekan jumped on top of him. Brandon managed to grab his wrist as the knife came down again, but Commander Veekan was too strong. He gritted his teeth and pushed back with everything he had, but he knew it wasn't enough. The blade slowly descended toward his face.

Suddenly, the pressure ceased, and time slowed down as Commander Veekan's head came toward him. It was as if Commander Veekan intended to give him a helmet-to-helmet kiss, but as the two helmets made contact, Commander Veekan's head rolled off to the side and fell to the ground. Brandon found himself staring at the headless body of Commander Veekan, and beyond it stood Jack, sword in hand.

Brandon pushed the corpse off of him and said, "What is with you and decapitating people?"

"Hurry," his brother replied, as he scooped Brandon's gun off the ground and tossed it to him.

As Brandon stood up he said, "Seriously man, I think you may need to seek professional help. You know the company has therapists that are supposed to be available to us at all times. Free of cost, too."

Jack ignored him, scooped up his own gun and began firing at the crowd again. Brandon joined him and followed suit. Only now there were even more ground forces moving in on them, and they were closer than before. Fortunately, they hadn't had a clear enough view beyond Commander Veekan's wreckage to feel comfortable charging in, or the brothers would already be dead.

Now gun fire rained in on them from every direction. Most of the mercs and bounty hunters had been pushed back, and the assassins were again competing with one another for the million-credit hit. The ground was a killing field, and Brandon was the star of the show.

The laser fire became so heavy that they were no longer able to fire back. The smell of burning metal filled the air, and he wondered how long the steel canister would hold up. He could only imagine that the continuous laser fire was slowly burning through it.

Just when the situation couldn't seem anymore hopeless, a giant warship fell out of the sky. It was solid black, sleek, yet large. It wasn't like a military personnel carrier, but amongst mid-class ships it was possibly the largest. Its cannons alone were bigger than Brandon's whole ship. He recognized it immediately. Anyone in the company would have recognized that ship. In fact they did, and immediately gave it plenty of room because this was the flagship of none other than Vice President Lynx Rufus. It was appropriately named The Warlord.

Brandon was surprised to see it, and he could tell that the other assassins were surprised to see it, too, when they stopped shooting at him and stared at the sky. They were even more surprised when The Warlord opened fire on them. Brandon had never seen nor imagined seeing a single warship unleash so much havoc. Even as it blasted other ships out of the sky it was scorching the earth. Every ship in the immediate vicinity attempted to flee. The ground soldiers attempted to find cover, but there wasn't much to be had. In a matter of seconds, Brandon was convinced that he and his brother were the only living creatures left on the ground.

The Warlord descended to the ground facing the brothers, and a cargo ramp opened. The armor-clad walking tank that was their Vice President stepped down the ramp, glanced toward them, and said, "Hurry."

As the VP turned and reentered his ship, the two brother raced after him. As soon as they cleared the ramp, the door shut behind them, and the ship lifted off the ground.

Brandon turned to Vice President Lynx Rufus and said, "Hey

Pops!"

The VP stared at Brandon for a moment and said, "You've got yourself in quite the mess, son."

CHAPTER TWELVE

"You never mentioned that this was our ride," Brandon said.

Jack shrugged in reply.

Brandon turned back toward the Vice President and said, "So how's it going, Dad? I didn't figure that you would want to get involved in this mess."

"One of my boys gets a hit put out on him, and you don't think I'm going to get involved?"

Vice President Lynx Rufus, or The Bobcat, had been the greatest assassin in the galaxy in his younger days. He had ascended through ranks in the company until he was the Vice President of the Kazor Sect. His real name, unknown to many, was Halcard Daivik, and though he was at one time the most feared man in the galaxy, he was also a loving husband and father to two sons. The eldest son of course had followed in his father's footsteps and had taken on the mantle of greatest assassin in the galaxy. The younger son had more or less stumbled along in his father's footsteps and blundered his way through the assassin business until becoming the most hunted man in the galaxy.

Of course, this was the main reason that both Brandon and Jack had gone to the trouble of lying to the company about their real identities. There was no shortage of scum-fucking assholes that would go after Halcard's children to get to him, so when Jack had joined Assassins Inc., Halcard had used his resources to help him a acquire a fake name. When Brandon had decided to join the company, he wasn't sure how his Dad would feel about it, so he went to Jack for help instead. Of course Jack had helped, but he had been stuck with the name Philup Mecrevice.

Halcard removed his helmet, and Brandon winced at the years on his father's face. Outside of an official capacity, which usually wasn't in person, he didn't see his father very often. The patch over his eye had in fact been paid for by the company, but not like the rumors Rego had mentioned at the meeting. It had been a fairly standard Worker's Compensation Claim. The company went a little extra distance to help him secure a state-of-the-art cyborg eye, but he was after all their greatest assassin and a high-ranking officer. He had lost it in battle, but he wouldn't ever say how. Halcard didn't talk about things like that. In fact, as a general rule, when they were at home the assassin business wasn't mentioned. Halcard could have been a telemarketer himself, the way he acted around the house. Brandon's mother wasn't a fan of his father's career, despite the fact he was extremely wealthy. This was why she had freaked out so bad when Jack had joined, and why Brandon had gone out of his way to make sure that she didn't know he had joined, too.

Jack broke through his thoughts saying, "Do we have any information on who put this hit out?"

Halcard shook his head and turned to Brandon, "No. I was hoping you might know something."

"I don't have a clue," Brandon said with a shrug. "I was hoping you might know something."

Halcard rubbed his greying beard and said, "No. As soon as the name Brandon Daivik hit the system, Raxle Naste reported to Human Resources that I had a son by that name. When Human Resources did a double check with my name, they knew you were my son. I was temporarily removed from my station, and it was strongly suggested to me that I take a personal leave of absence."

"Wow," Brandon said.

Halcard nodded. "Raxle Naste has been given temporary control of Kazor Sect. The only good news is that HR said it would be considered understandable if I took action to rescue you, and that they wouldn't hold it against me as long as I was on leave and didn't use company resources in an attempt to rescue you. Based on the situation below, it's apparent that they have also figured out that Agkistrodon is Brandon Daivik."

Brandon shook his head in disbelief. "I'm sorry, Pops. Do you think Raxle Naste planned this? Do you think it was his way of securing power?"

Halcard shook his head. "I don't think so. He is one sly little fox, but he knows he's got to be careful around this old bobcat. It's possible I suppose, but I don't think it's likely. Raxle is more of a creature of opportunity than a prudent planner."

"Then who?" Brandon asked. "Because I've got nothing."

"Who have you pissed off recently?" Jack asked.

Brandon thought about it for a moment and said, "The entire company with the carrots ordeal. And I imagine that all of the people that Rharo Staris owed money to weren't too happy with me executing him. Oh and the floor manager of the casino wasn't too pleased with me and I heard he got fired. Also, I'm a few months behind on rent. Which of course was why my best pal Rego betrayed me."

Halcard shook his head. "We can obviously rule out your land-lord. I doubt the casino floor manager would have enough money to order this kind of hit, or he wouldn't have been a floor manager in the first place. If the people who Rharo Staris owed money were mad that they weren't going to be able to get their money back, I don't see them putting up even more money to kill you for killing him. Nothing fits."

"You don't think it was the company?" Brandon asked.

His father shook his head. "No, there's no way our CEO would approve that kind of an expense. It's not even remotely possible. Not unless someone else in the company put up money person-ally. The only one that I can think of would be Raxle, and I still don't think it's him, though he is certainly becoming a problem."

"You'll get your job back, Pops," Brandon said.

"That's not what I was referring to," Halcard said. "Wait... You don't know yet?"

"Know what?"

"You better check your personal communication account."

Brandon did. Using the display options within his helmet he brought up his communication accounts. There was a new vid message from an Unknown Source on both accounts, and it was only a half hour old. He started the video, and the screen filled his vision.

Horror clutched him when he realized what he was looking at. It was Naria, and she was in restraints. Behind her stood none other than Director Raxle Naste. He smiled at the camera and said, "Hello Brandon, or should I say Agkistrodon? I hope this message finds you in good health. As you are now aware, there has been a sizable hit placed on your head. You have been with Assassins Incorporated long enough to know that we all must make sacrifices for the company... Some greater than others. You will immediately set course for the coordinates set in this communication. There you will board my personal ship, The Macair. You will do so unarmed and will offer no resistance when my men take you into custody. Then you will be executed in a painless and dignified fashion. Your execution will of course be broadcasted directly to the client."

He paused for a moment smiling at the camera, and added, "Oh, and Brandon, if I even so much as think The Warlord has entered my space or that your father is anywhere near... Well...

Let's just say that your woman will make the sacrifice for you."

At this Naria screamed, "Don't do it Brandon! Don't worry about me! Just run! Get as far away as you..."

Raxle Naste put his hand over Naria's mouth and gently brushed the top of her head, "Shh dear, there's no reason to get excited. I would hate to see you wind up dead and demoted. Remember, this is for the benefit of the company."

Naria burst into tears, and Raxle Naste smiled at the camera. "I hope to be seeing you very soon, Brandon."

The vid ended, and Brandon switched off his communicator. Turning back toward his father and brother, he said, "I'll kill that son of a bitch. If he hurts Naria there won't be enough assassins in the galaxy to stop me."

"Calm down," his father said.

"The hell with that," Brandon spat. "Tell your pilot to set course. I'm going to get my girlfriend back."

"You'll just get yourself killed," Jack said.

"Yeah, so what's your point?"

"I just risked my neck to save you, and I'm not going to watch you throw your life away," Jack said.

"He has Naria," Brandon spat through gritted teeth.

"Boys," their father said, with the tone that still made them both wince, "bickering will not help us solve this problem. We need to come up with a plan. That requires using your damn heads like I raised you. Now think, dammit!"

"What can we do other than exactly what he said? It's not like we even know who put the hit out on me!"

Before anyone replied, another voice came over the comm speaker. "Commander Rufus, we are clear of the atmosphere. Would you like me to set a destination?"

Halcard replied, "We're on our way up."

Halcard headed toward the front of the ship with his two sons falling in line behind him. Brandon had never been on The Warlord, but he had often wondered what it was like inside. Rego and his other acquaintances in the company always speculated that it was lavished with the finest furnishings and latest tech. Brandon knew better. As long as it involved the job, then they were probably right about the tech, but his father wasn't one for fine furnishings. Despite his great wealth, he was a simple kind of man. He didn't believe in over spending on non-necessities. There was no telling how much he had spent on the ship, but it was a tool and it had a purpose. The ship was not only a symbol to the assassins of Kazor Sect, but it was one of the meanest ships in space.

As they walked through the sleek hallways Brandon noticed that there was an exceptionally large crew and he asked, "If you aren't allowed to be using company resources then why are all of these people here?"

Without turning back to look at him, his father continued walking and said, "The crew of The Warlord all work for me. I pay their wages, not the company. My ship. My crew."

Brandon nodded and continued following until they were in the cockpit. It had seating for six and plenty of standing room. A humanoid with one eye turned toward them as they approached and said, "We're prepared to jump to light speed as soon as you give us the destination, Commander. We seem to be safe for the moment. The other ships are giving us a wide berth."

"Are they still trying to hail us?" Halcard asked.

"Yes sir, several of them are. More have tried to apply sneaky tracking hacks into the system. We have isolated them all and prepared to remove them as soon as we are ready to leave."

Halcard nodded and replied, "That gives me an idea. Do we still have any of the Vertan reverse mani-transmitters?"

The one eyed man nodded. "Yes sir. We've only just received the newest models from the labs. There isn't a system on the planet that should be able to notice them."

Brandon didn't know what they were talking about, but besides being an assassin, Halcard also owned the largest Assassin tech company in the galaxy. Vertan made top of the line tech and equipment that every assassin in the galaxy wanted to purchase. Of course quality products meant high prices, and most assassins, Brandon included, couldn't afford their gear.

Halcard seemed to be nodding to himself deep in thought. Brandon knew the look. It meant the old man was trying to solve their problems. Brandon left him with his thoughts and stared out at what should have been dark, empty space but instead was filled with numerous ships. Some of them he even recognized, but most he didn't.

Halcard broke through his thoughts saying, "We need to get a Vertan reverse mani-transmitter on Raxle's ship."

Jack nodded, because of course he knew what Halcard was talking about. "It won't be easy. He's certainly prepared for an attack. Sneaking on to the ship would be a challenge."

"There must be a way," Halcard said. "It's our best chance to figure this thing out."

"What the hell are you guys talking about?" Brandon asked. "What the hell is a Vertan reverse whatever transmitter?"

"Sorry, son, it's a device for hacking and tracking connections. Raxle Naste said that the client for the hit would be watching the execution. That means that the client has a connection to Raxle's ship. If we can get one of these devices onto his ship's system, then we can potentially track the connection and find out who the client is."

Brandon nodded. "I like it, but how?"

"We could use one of the Vertan 8J4600 Artificial Life Imitators. Do you still have any onboard?" Jack asked.

Halcard nodded. "Perhaps there's a way we could use one."

"Again guys," Brandon said, "I am lost. Remember, I'm much too poor to be able to afford anything with the name Vertan on it."

"They're robots," Halcard said, "that look and move like a human. They even have human heads and wear armor just like an assassin. They don't hold up forever, though. On close inspection it's pretty obvious that they aren't human. It wouldn't distract Raxle Naste long."

"Long enough to set off one of the self-destruct sequences and take out Naxle Raste," Jack said.

"But that won't save Naria," Brandon said.

"And it won't help us find out who ordered this hit," Halcard said. "We need to get a mani-transmitter on board and locked into their communication system."

"And Raxle Naste's invitation was for one," Brandon said, "so it's not like more than one person can go. Can you think of anything?"

"I don't know." Halcard shook his head, and then turned to the one-eyed alien. "Go ahead and kill the tracking hacks. Let's get some place safer where we can come up with a solid plan."

Brandon was staring back out the window again, and suddenly yelled, "Wait! Belay that order! I have an idea!"

Everyone in the cockpit stared at him. Jack folded his arms over his chest and said, "This ought to be great."

"Shut up," Brandon said. Turning to the one-eyed man said, "Can you make it look like you were trying to get rid of one of the hacks but failed?"

"Easy," the man replied with a shrug.

Halcard slapped the man on the back and said, "Zeef here is one the smartest tech heads in the galaxy. There isn't too much that he couldn't do. What do you have in mind?"

"Okay," Brandon said, "I recognize one of those ships out there. We're going to go to the Falton Cluster, and I want to make sure that they track us there."

"The Falton Cluster?" Jack said. "But that's pretty much just an asteroid field. Good hiding spot, but what good is having them track us there going to do?"

"I want them to catch me... Obviously."

CHAPTER THIRTEEN

"Well you got us," Lenis said as soon as the airlock opened. The bounty hunter's arms were crossed, and she was fully geared out in her armor. "First you assassinate my bounty, and now you've got the most feared warship in the galaxy with its weapons pointed at my ship. You never cease to impress me, Agkistrodon."

"Well you may be the only one," he replied as he stepped into the cargo bay of her ship.

"I noticed you down there amongst the trash," Lenis said. "Sure seemed like you were the center of attention. Looked like all of your assassin buddies were gunning for you. Am I to assume that you're the target?"

Brandon spread his hands and laughed. "You've got it."

"Who the hell did you piss you off?"

Brandon shrugged in reply. Behind Lenis, her team was spread out, weapons ready. Surprised mumbles went up around the room as Naja Ashei and Lynx Rufus stepped in behind him. If the bounty hunters weren't nervous before, they certainly were now. That was exactly what he wanted.

"You certainly keep interesting company," Lenis said.

Brandon gave her shrug.

"So how'd you do it?" she asked.

He wished she could see the smile behind his helmet. He let her stand there for a moment and finally said, "We made sure that your tracking hack appeared to be working. Then we flew here, dumped the transmitter you were locked onto, and hid behind a giant rock until you showed up. You know the rest."

Lenis nodded. "And here I thought you were coming to this system to hide behind an asteroid to avoid the rest of galaxy, turns out it was only me that you were hiding from. If you wanted to kill us, The Warlord's weapons could easily turn my ship into dust. So what do you want?"

"I want to hire you."

"First you steal my bounty, which impressed me, but then you got paid in carrots. That made me think that you were pretty much a complete idiot. Then you catch me with my pants down like this, and I start to think you're pretty clever again. Now you say you want to hire me, despite knowing that I've obviously been hunting you down to kill you along with the rest of the galaxy." She paused then finally said, "You're either a complete moron, or the smartest bastard in the galaxy."

Brandon chuckled. "Your part in trying to kill me is over."

"Is it?"

"Yes," he replied. "You don't have to agree to take my job offer, but you are done hunting me, because if you continue hunting me then we will blow your ship and everyone in it out of the sky."

Lenis nodded. "Fair enough. I don't care much for this assassination business anyway. Wouldn't have even set out on it if the Bounty Hunters Association hadn't demanded it. It's a lot of money, but way too many problems, getting blown out of the sky being at the top of the list."

"Good," Brandon said. "The job I have in mind for you is more in line with what you bounty hunters normally do anyway."

Lenis stared at him for a moment and said, "How dangerous is it?"

"There's a good chance we're all going to get killed," Brandon said with a shrug.

There were mumbles from her people, but one cross look from Lenis shut them up. She turned back to Brandon and asked, "What's the pay?"

His father answered. "One hundred thousand credits now. Another hundred thousand when the job's done and we're alive."

Murmurs went up from Lenis's team again, but this time she didn't bother to silence them. Instead she said, "That's a lot of money. What's the job?"

Brandon laughed. "I want you turn me over to Assassins Incorporated."

"Yup, just what I thought," Lenis said. "You're a complete moron."

CHAPTER FOURTEEN

"Are you sure this is going to work?" Lenis asked.

"Not even a little bit," Brandon said. "But if it works you'll get paid and I'll find out who put the hit on me. I just hope your team is as good as you say they are."

"They are. We'll do our part. And I'm not worried about Naja Ashei. I'm more worried about you."

"Thanks for the vote of confidence."

Lenis's ship dropped out of light speed and there was The Macair, the personal flagship of Raxle Naste. It wasn't sleek and meant for the job like his father's. Raxle Naste's ship was a large and bulky warship. A military model meant to hold a large amount of people and several smaller ships. It was completely impractical for an assassin, but Raxle Naste wasn't really an assassin anymore. For the past several years he was a figure head, and his large ship was meant to stand as a symbol of his power. Of course, everyone in the company secretly whispered that it was over compensation for his tiny prick.

Immediately one of Lenis's men hailed the larger ship and identified them as members of the Bounty Hunters Association. A few moments later a voice replied, "What's your business here Bounty Hunters?"

Lenis replied, "We wish to speak to Director Raxle Naste."

"Director Naste is busy," replied the voice. "He doesn't simply take calls from just anyone."

"Tell him that it involves the big hit that everyone is after," Lenis said, replying in the same disdainful tone.

The voice practically spat. "State your purpose clearly. I need to know why you would be calling him about this particular issue."

Lenis chuckled. "We have the target."

"Please hold," said the voice.

A few moments later the voice of Raxle Naste said, "This is acting Vice President Raxle Naste. How may I assist you?"

Lenis glanced over at Brandon, and then said, "This is Lenis Formoon with the Bounty Hunter's Association. I'm reaching out to you about the hit on Brandon Daivik."

"Am I to understand that you've secured Mr. Daivik?"

"That is correct."

"Interesting," Raxle Naste said. "So why would you be bringing him here rather than simply executing the contract yourself?"

"We were about to when the target began begging for his life. He is quite the pathetic little creature and maybe he was just trying to buy himself more time. However, he explained that there might be more than just money to be gained by reaching out to you."

"How so?"

"Look, I'll be honest with you. My team and I have felt a little overlooked in the Bounty Hunters Association. We feel like we are all deserving of higher rank, but politics have held us back. We've collectively considered applying to Assassins Inc., but have been concerned with starting over at a lower level, pay, and benefits. If you'll agree to compensate us for fifty percent of this commission, give us at least a lateral position within Assassins Inc., a ten percent pay bump to what each of us are currently making, and ensure we have equal benefits, then we will turn Mr. Daivik over to you, and you will be able to claim your part in securing the hit and you get twenty five percent of the commission. Best of all you will be the person that ensured that Assassins Incorporated made the hit, rather than the Bounty Hunters Association."

"That is an interesting offer," Raxle Naste said. "After what happened to team Senrath, I could use another good team. Does your team have a resume?"

"I'll upload it now."

"Thank you," Raxle Naste said. "Give me a few minutes to consider your offer, and I shall circle back around with a response."

The communication clicked off and Lenis glanced over at Brandon. "You know the guy better than me. Do you think he bought it?"

Askistrodon started to say, "Hard to..."

The ship communicator buzzed and Lenis answered it saying, "This is Commander Formoon."

"Miss Formoon, I've considered your offer."

"That didn't take long."

Raxle Naste chuckled. "Let me be the first to welcome you to Assassins Incorporated. Your requests are reasonable, and I feel that you and your associates would make a great addition to our team-spirited environment. My men will let you know which bay to dock your ship in. I look forward to meeting you in person."

"Likewise," Lenis replied.

When the communication ended, Lenis turned to Brandon and said, "I hope this plan of yours works."

"Not as much as I do."

CHAPTER FIFTEEN

The bay they docked in was rather small, and theirs was the only ship, which didn't make Brandon feel better about the plan at all. There were, however, approximately thirty guards in grey armor to welcome them. Lenis wasted no time in strolling out to meet them. Eight members of her team followed behind her, pushing their captive forward. They were all fully armored and armed, including Lenis. The remaining four members of her team were left behind to guard the ship.

One of the guards stepped forward and said, "Are you sure the prisoner is bound securely?"

"Those are bintanium laser gauntlets. He's secure," Lenis said. Then she added, "We're bounty hunters; this is what we do."

The guard nodded. "Fair enough. I will lead you to Vice President Raxle Naste."

"I thought he was a director," Lenis replied.

"He has assumed the role of Vice President for the time being," replied the guard. "Follow me."

Half of the guards led the way, while the other half fell in step behind Lenis's team.

Brandon's stomach was in knots. There was a no backing out now; if his plan failed he was dead.

As they marched out of the bay, no one noticed a dark armored figure slither into the shadows.

They were led to a large room with a giant screen. Before it stood Raxle Naste with even more of his private guards. Corporate espionage was always a concern, and the company didn't skimp on protection for the higher ups. To Naste, the guards were nothing more than another status symbol, just like his giant warship.

Off to one side of the room was Naria. Her hands were bound, and her mouth was covered with some kind of device that Brandon could only assume was to keep her silent. As she saw them enter the room, she attempted to move and one of the guards immediately restrained her. As the guard held her, tears began streaming down her face.

Only half of their guard escort remained. They took position on either side of Lenis's team. They stood at ease, but their weapons remained in hand, and it was clear they were prepared for trouble.

Behind Raxle Naste was a large, black screen. It gave a light glow, indicating that it was on, but Brandon could not quite put a finger on its purpose.

Raxle Naste smiled as they approached and said, "Welcome!"

He strode forward and shook hands with Lenis. "I welcome you to my ship, and to Assassins Incorporated!"

"Thank you," Lenis replied.

"I can assure you that you've made the right move," Raxle Naste said. "You will have a bright future with us."

"That's what we're hoping for."

"So this is our man, eh?" Raxle Naste said, as he stepped past Lenis. "Let's move him to the center here so he has a clear line of sight in front of the camera."

As Brandon was moved to the center of the room and pushed to his knees, he asked, "What about Naria?"

"She'll be unharmed. We are not monsters. Just business-men. You should understand," Raxle Naste said. Then he turned to face Lenis. "The client is watching this via a direct feed. Here at Assassins Incorporated customer service is our number one priority. You will learn about that in orientation."

"I'm sure," Lenis replied.

He strolled toward the screen and said, "If you are ready, I don't see any reason in delaying further."

In a large bold print a response came across the screen. "Please remove his helmet so that we may ensure accuracy."

"Of course," Raxle Naste said.

He quickly stepped over and began removing Agkistrodon's helmet. It only took a few moments to reveal the human face below. He stepped away so that the camera could see the face, and said, "See, as we promised, we make good on all of our hits."

The screen didn't immediately reply, and Raxle Naste turned to one of his men. "The serum."

The guard immediately pulled a long needle out of a black case and passed it on to Raxle Naste. He held the needle out, and glanced back up at the screen. "Once injected, the subject will immediately begin to lose motor function. In a matter of minutes his heart beat will slow to a crawl, and then he will die. It's a special blend that my very own researchers concocted and includes a large dose of pain inhibitors and muscle relaxers so that the subject feels no pain."

The word "wait" came across the screen.

"Is there a problem?" Raxle Naste said to the screen.

The screen replied, "That's not Brandon Daivik."

Raxle Naste glanced back at the figure on the floor, and then pulled the dossier on his wrist communication device. A large picture of the target appeared in front of his face. He glanced at the picture and back at the target, and then said, "It appears to be him to me."

The screen replied, "That's not him. I assure you."

Raxle turned toward Lenis. "What's going on here!?"

Hidden amongst Lenis's bounty hunters, the real Agkistrodon cursed to himself, and glanced at his doppelganger robot in the center of the room. They hadn't had time to get the face perfect, but most people wouldn't have immediately known the difference. This made him only more curious about the client, but now wasn't the time to worry about that. He had hoped to give Jack more time to install the transmitter device, but it appeared that the game was nearly up.

Lenis said, "I don't know what you're talking about. This is Brandon Daivik. Look at him."

Raxle Naste's eyes glanced down at the captive figure and glanced up at the screen again. "You are sure this isn't him?"

"Yes," replied the screen. "It's a close replica, but that is not Brandon Daivik."

Raxle Naste turned hate-filled eyes toward Lenis. Every eye in the room turned toward Lenis. Fortunately, that meant that none of the eyes were falling on the random bounty hunter standing near the back of the group. The real Brandon had borrowed a suit of armor from Lenis's crew, and he looked like he belonged with them. Which was why no one had suspected anything of him, and why no one was looking his way when he moved his hand to the little button on his belt.

Jack would certainly curse him for being rushed, but the game was up. There were precious seconds to waste before Raxle Naste ordered them all shot to death. It was time to move. He pressed the button.

As soon as he did, the fake Brandon's eyes and mouth lit up with bright red light. A moment later his head exploded. It wasn't a large explosion; Brandon hadn't wanted to harm Naria or any of Lenis's team. It did have enough impact to send Raxle Naste flying to the floor. Then purple smoke started pouring from the neck hole and filling the room. Most quality helmets had night vision and infrared options, but his father had explained that this new prototype smoke would block them out. To see through it required a special lens which Halcard had made sure they were all equipped with beforehand. This meant that everyone in the room was blind except for Brandon and Lenis's team.

As they had discussed, they immediately spread out, crouched low, and began taking out guards.

Brandon yelled through the communicator in his helmet, "The Copperhead has struck! I repeat! The Copperhead has struck!"

One of Lenis's men who was waiting at the ship replied, "Acknowledged. Prepping the Eagle to fly."

The voice of his brother replied, "The Cobra is in range to envenom... Why did you come up with these stupid things to say? Our lines our coded anyway. No one can hear us."

"Quit yer bitchin' and hurry up, Naja," Brandon said. "The frog is in the frying pan!"

"You're an idiot," his brother replied.

Brandon worked his way toward Naria, carefully staying low to avoid getting shot. Raxle Naste was yelling orders, but through the smoke Brandon could see that he was fleeing out a side door. He tried to get a shot at the bastard, but there were too many bodies in the way, and Naria was his first priority.

There was a guard still holding her, but he was blinded, so he didn't see it when Brandon rammed a laser knife through his visor. Naria let out a yelp as the man fell behind her. Brandon put his knife away and took her by the bindings on her wrist.

He leaned in close and said, "Naria, it's me, Brandon. I'm going to lead you out of here, but I need you to crouch low so you don't get shot."

She gave a small nod in reply, and they headed for the exit where the bounty hunters were slowly congregating. Most of the guards were dead now, but a few were still taking pot shots into the purple fog.

As they ran into the hall, the voice of Raxle Naste came over the ship's speakers. "We have hostiles on the ship! Lock down all areas and begin emergency protocols! I want every one of those bastards taken out!"

Doors on both ends of the hall suddenly slammed down and

locked with a hiss.

"Dammit!" Brandon bellowed.

"I thought Naja Ashei was supposed to be handling this for us," Lenis spat. "We're dead if we don't get out of here quick."

"He is," Brandon said, and added. "He'll come through. He never fails at anything."

"That's the rumor," Lenis said.

"That's the reality," Brandon said. "He's never failed at anything in his whole life, smug bastard."

Before Lenis could reply the lights suddenly went out, and they could clearly hear the hiss of one of the doors unlocking and reopening. The bounty hunters immediately raised their weapons.

"See?" Brandon said, as he started moving down the open hallway. "Naria, stay in the middle of us, and keep your head down."

Again she nodded her reply.

Jack's icy voice cut through the main channel so that the entire team could hear him. "I've disabled main ship power and power to their door locks. Everything is open leading back to the ship. Everything else will stay on lockdown until they find a way to override the system. I've also cut power to their shield generator, cannons, and all other ship defense systems."

Halcard's voice came through and said, "Acknowledged. The bobcat is moving in to pounce... Seriously, Agkistrodon? These are the best codes you could come up with?"

Brandon ignored his father and said, "Naja, how long do we have?"

"At the minimum it will take five minutes for them to get full systems on line."

Halcard cut in. "Plenty of time for The Warlord to destroy the ship."

"We're still on here, you know?" Brandon said.

"Then hurry," was his father's response. "I've waited a long time for this day. It's high time that I show Raxle Naste what a real assassin's ship can do."

Brandon said, "Naja, did you plant the mani-transmitter thing?"

"Yes," Jack replied.

"Zeef is already working on tracking the signal," Halcard said. "Hurry."

Jack said, "Meet you guys on the ship."

Brandon looked back at the others and said, "We'd better pick up the pace."

CHAPTER SIXTEEN

They were met with little resistance as they headed back toward the ship. Once they turned a corner and found themselves faced with two of Raxle Naste's men. Brandon gunned down the first before he had a chance to raise his weapon. Lenis killed the second as he was taking aim. Beyond that, their trip back to the dock was uneventful.

Just before they entered the ship bay there was a large thud, and the whole ship rocked as if it had just been hit with an earthquake. Brandon and company were slammed against the walls, but all managed to stay on their feet. Moments later it happened again, and Brandon knew beyond any doubt that his father's ship was on the attack.

As soon as they entered the bay, lasers started flying toward them. Every side door in the bay began to open, and Assassins Incorporated employees began pouring out. They swarmed the bay like ants and immediately set to blocking their path to the ship.

Brandon and company dove behind some cargo crates for cover, but it was barely enough for all of them to squeeze behind. The ship was some forty yards away, and more assassins were filling the space in between by the second.

"You have a plan for this part!?" Lenis asked.

Brandon nodded. "Yeah, kill everyone that's trying to kill us!"

"That's your plan?" Lenis spat. "There I was starting to think you were clever again, and you totally turned it around."

Brandon shrugged. "Exit strategies have never been my strong point."

Lenis growled and joined her men in shooting at the swarm of assassins. Brandon followed suit and peaked his head over the crate along with his rifle. The good news was that there were so many of them that he almost didn't have to aim. He immediately set to work gunning down his fellow Assassins Inc. employees.

The remaining members of the bounty hunter team from the ship began opening fire from the bay door, but they had little impact on the horde.

Suddenly his communicator started buzzing that he had an

incoming call. He crawled back down into cover, and pulled up the communicator display in his helmet. The call was on his personal account and it was his mom. He chose the ignore call button, and leaned back out to shoot.

Suddenly a voice in his head said, "Brandon."

He paused and said, "Mom!?"

"Yeah it's me," she said. "I guess it's hard for you to remember who I am given that you never answer or return my calls."

"This really isn't a good time right now, Mom."

"Well you are just going to have to make it a good time!"

"Seriously Mom! I will call you back as soon as I can, but I can't talk right now. I shouldn't have even answered."

"You didn't answer!" she said, with venom coursing through her words. "Since you continued to ignore my calls, I had your father's company make me a way to force your communicator to answer."

"You did what!?"

"Yeah, that's right son! And it's pretty sad that a mother would have to do that!"

"Mom, I will call you right back. I seriously need to go!"

Out of the corner of his helmet he saw an assassin trying to slip around the crates. He quickly aimed and fired, sending a laser bolt through the assassin's chest.

"I cannot believe I have raised a son with such disregard for his mother!"

"I'm not disregarding you! I'm just in the middle of something!"

"Where did I go wrong?" she said. "I tried to be a good mother."

"You are a great mom," he said, as he shot another assassin.

"Oh, don't patronize me son," she said. "I carried you for nine months."

"I know mom!" Brandon said. "Seriously, I've got to go!"

"Are you at work?"

"Wha... Yes... That's it. I'm at work. I've got an important sale on hold on another line. I really need to finish the call or my boss will be furious. And I'm not supposed to take personal calls while I'm working."

"Well I'm sure that if your boss knew how long it had been since you called your mother..."

"I tried to call you just a few hours ago!" he yelled. "You didn't answer!"

"Well, I was busy," she said. "And don't take that tone with me, boy! I'm your mother!"

A grenade flew overhead and landed right in the middle of their group. Before it had time to blow, Lenis dove, grabbed it, hurled it back over the crate, and screamed, "Grenade!!!"

They all ducked as the grenade exploded in the air just a few feet past the crates.

"Brandon what is all of that background noise?" his mother asked.

Brandon glanced around him. Gunfire was roaring through the room, along with the occasional scream or the boom of a grenade. On top of that, The Warlord's constant barrage was tearing the ship apart. He didn't have a reasonable explanation to give her.

"Are you playing games!? You're too busy to talk to me because you are playing your damn graphic simulator games! Unbelievable!" she screamed.

"Yeah," he said, not sure what else he could say. "I'm playing games."

"You pause it this instant and talk to your mother!"

"I can't pause it," he said. "I'm playing through galac-net with other people. You can't pause when you're playing with other people. Besides my team is counting on me!"

"Yeah, well you just tell those other people that you're talking to your mother! I'm sure they all talk to their mothers on regular basis!"

"Mom, I will call you right back!"

"I just think it's funny how you find the time for everyone else, but you can't find time for me!"

"Mom..."

"Amazing! I carry you for nine months, raise you to be a loving son, then you become an adult and ignore me completely!"

"Mom!"

"I hope Naria knows how you treat your mother. You know they say that the way a man treats his mother is how he will treat his wife!"

"Mother! Stop!"

"Ohhh!!!" Her pitch turned into angry squeal. "How dare you!!! You don't tell me to stop!!! You don't tell your own fucking mother to stop!!! No son of mine will speak to me that way!!!"

"You are acting crazy right now!" Brandon said. "I love you, but you need to calm down!"

"Oh I'll calm down alright! You ungrateful little shit! After everything I've done for you!"

"Mom!"

"Goodbye, Brandon! I Hope you have a good time playing with your friends," she said, through obviously gritted teeth. "I hope they love you as much as your mother does! Oh, and I say *Brandon*, because obviously you aren't my son. No son of mine would talk to me that way! Goodbye!"

"Bye, Mom, love ya," he said as he continued firing over the crate.

She ended the connection, and he sighed with relief.

Beside him Lenis asked, "Was that your mom?"

"Yeah."

"Wow," she said. "I could hear her through your helmet and over all the gun fire."

"Yeah," Brandon said. "She's a special kind of crazy sometimes."

"Well if you're done with your little chat, we've got to find a way out of here."

Brandon leaned over the box again to assess the situation, and jumped back down saying, "That might not be an option anymore."

"Why?"

"Because your men that stayed with the ship have closed the door, and it appears that they are firing it up."

"What!?"

"Yeah, I think they are leaving us."

"My men wouldn't do that!"

Just as she finished her statement the ship lifted off the ground.

"Are you sure?" he asked. "Cause it really looks like they are bailing on us."

Brandon was proved immediately wrong as the ship tilted down and began using its laser beams to pepper the bay.

"What are they doing?" Lenis cried.

It wasn't hard to figure out why she was losing it. There was just enough room in the bay to land ships. If anything broke the pressure seal, everyone would die. Whoever was flying the ship was doing it with expert precision.

The ship suddenly tilted to the side and began moving toward them. Just before it smashed into the crates the ship came to a stop and landed. The bay door opened and one of the bounty hunters leaned out and said, "Hurry!"

None of them needed further encouragement; they ran to the ship. As soon as everyone was on the ship the doors closed and they took off.

"Damn, Lenis!" Brandon said. "You have one hell of a pilot."

Lenis pointed at the bounty hunter that had opened the door. "This is my pilot."

"Then who the hell is flying..." He didn't have to finish. He already knew the answer. "Smug bastard is flying the ship. How the hell did he beat us?"

"I don't know," Lenis's pilot said. "I always swore I would never let anyone else fly her, but you can't really say no to Naja Ashei."

Brandon just shook his head and moved to the front of the ship. Jack was sitting in the cockpit and speeding the bounty hunters' ship towards The Warlord. From the outside he could clearly see that Raxle Naste's ship was in much worse shape than he had realized. The assault was taking a heavy toll, and Brandon knew that it wouldn't hold up much longer.

As if reading his thoughts Jack said, "There won't be much left of the The Macair in a few minutes."

Brandon nodded, and watched as escape pods ejected and smaller ships zipped away to escape from the ruined ship.

"You think Raxle Naste made it off?" Brandon asked.

Jack shrugged. "Hard to say, but I imagine that bastard headed for the nearest ship the moment The Warlord opened fire."

Brandon nodded again and watched the flames consuming the larger ship. Still The Warlord didn't let up, and after a few more seconds the entire ship exploded. Raxle Naste's flagship was no more.

CHAPTER SEVENTEEN

"Yes... Mmhmm... I agree completely," Halcard was saying as Brandon entered his father's private chamber on the ship. He held a finger to his lips and said, "I will have a talk with him, dear... Yes I completely agree... I said I will have a talk with him... Yes dear, I love you, too."

Halcard turned to his son and said, "You've really pissed your mother off this time."

"What was I supposed to do?" Brandon said. "I was in the middle of trying not get my head shot off."

"Well she thinks you were ignoring her for a game."

"I know, but there wasn't much else I could say. Can you imagine how she would have reacted if I told her I've been lying to her all this time, that I'm actually an assassin, and oh by the way everyone in the galaxy is out to get me? Aren't you the one who told me ignorance is bliss?"

Halcard shook his head. "When this is all over with, you had better go spend some time with your mother."

"I know, and I will," Brandon said, and then to change the subject asked, "Did the transmitter work?"

"It picked up the trail, but it's still attempting to decode and triangulate the exact location. We should have a fix within an hour or so."

"Perfect," Brandon said. "Do you have a way to override Naria's bonds? It's a Nanite5000 model."

Halcard nodded. "Of course, and I've set up a private bunk room for you. Once you get her taken care of get some rest. As soon as we have a fix on the location I'll contact you."

"Thanks, Dad," Brandon said. "I appreciate you doing all of this for me."

Halcard gave him a little nod, and said, "Did you really think I wouldn't? You're my son."

The moment he had her bounds removed Naria tackled him in a hug. Had he not been wearing his armor, she might have squeezed the air right out of him. They held each other for a moment, and then she slowly removed his helmet. Once it was clear they slid into a deep kiss. It lasted for several seconds, and he wasn't sure that he ever wanted to stop.

When she pulled away he said, "God I was so worried about you."

"I thought you were going to sacrifice yourself for me. I was so scared."

"Well I was," he admitted, "but we came up with a better plan."

She nodded. "I don't know what to say."

"You don't have to say anything, Naria. For the moment we're both safe. Everything is alright."

"How can you say that, Brandon? Everyone in the galaxy is trying to kill you."

"I know," he replied. "But right now none of that matters. Right now we're together, and that's all I care about."

"But for how long?"

"A while. It's going to take time to find out where the client is hiding. I don't know after that. I guess it depends who it is and where."

She gave him a devious smile again and said, "So we have some time? You're sure?"

"Yup."

"Take off your armor."

"You're the boss."

"Good," she said with a wink. "Then go take a shower, and come back to me."

"You don't want to join me?"

"Well, I guess you did just come rescue me," she said as she rose to join him.

"And this is now officially the best thing that's happened all day."

He re-entered the room wearing only a towel and suddenly felt overdressed. Naria was lying patiently in the bed, her clothes still in a pile on the floor alongside his own. They had made love twice in the shower, but he still felt a lump in his throat as he stared at her naked body.

As he approached, she stood and pushed him down on the bed. His heartbeat quickened as he stared at her. She moved over to him, threw her legs across his waist, and straddled him. The feeling of her weight pressed against his body immediately brought him to arousal. Her mouth was on his, and they were kissing slowly.

He pulled away and stared at her. "You're beautiful..."

She put a finger over his mouth and said, "Shhh, just lie back and close your eyes, my love."

He didn't need to be told twice and awkwardly waited with his eyes closed. After a few moments he felt her hands slide around him, and she said, "Just keep your eyes closed. I'll take care of everything."

She moved her hand slowly and he groaned. She giggled lightly in response. He could feel her weight moving over him again, and risked a peek. The first thing he noticed were her bare breasts staring back at him. The next thing he noticed was the hand raised over her head, and the glint of steel as the needle came down. He rolled to the left, and heard the poof as it struck the pillow. He rolled right again, knocking her to the floor.

She hit the ground with a grunt and immediately went for the side arm holstered to his discarded pants. Fortunately, it became tangled and he had just enough time to reach her before she could train it on him. He easily slapped it away and pushed her back to the floor.

He scooped the gun up himself, pointed it at her, and said, "What the hell, Naria!?"

From where she sat curled up naked on the floor she said, "It's a lot of money, Brandon."

"So even you're trying to kill me!?" Brandon said. "What the fuck, Naria!? I thought we had something special!"

"Oh don't be an idiot, Brandon," she said. "We were always just using each other. You think I was honestly falling for you? You were just a fling to pass the time. I don't like picking up random guys in bars. You were a cheap lay is all."

"Unbelievable!" he shouted. "I came to rescue you!"

"Rescue me? That just shows what an idiot you are." She laughed. "Who do you think came up with the idea in the first place? How do you suppose that Assassins Inc. found out that I was your girlfriend? Or for that matter, how do you think that Assassins Inc. found out that you were Agkistrodon?"

"I don't know," he spat. "I was too busy working out a plan to rescue you."

"You idiot," she said. "I was the one that approached Raxle Naste with a plan to make you come to us. He promised to promote me to a Senior Manager position. I knew that you were just romantic enough to try to sacrifice yourself to save me. Then you had to storm in there with an army and fuck the whole thing up. That's so typical of you."

"You bitch!" he said.

"Oh please," she said. "What now? Are you going to kill me?"

"I'm really fucking considering it," he said, and then kicked the restraints he had earlier removed toward her. "Put these back on."

She reached for the hand bonds and he said, "No, do the mouth thing first. I don't want to hear you speak."

CHAPTER EIGHTEEN

"So Naria was behind Raxle Naste's whole plan," Jack said, and with a sigh added, "Women."

Brandon nodded his agreement and sat down. They were in a small conference room. Their father had asked them to meet him there immediately, and Brandon had obliged, hoping that the transmitter device had proved useful.

Halcard appeared a moment later, his helmet discarded, rage spread across his face.

"What's wrong?" Brandon asked.

"The transmitter just finished tracking the signal from the client."

"Okay?"

"It came from my office," Halcard said.

"At Assassins Incorporated Headquarters?" Brandon asked.

"No," Halcard said. "At home."

Brandon and Jack shared a look, and Brandon said, "How is that possible?"

"That's not all," Halcard said. "We got this comm vid from Raxle Naste a minute ago."

He turned and fired up a screen on the wall. It was clearly Halcard's office at home. Brandon was sure. Sitting behind his father's desk was Raxle Naste.

He looked much the same as he had on his own ship a short time before, but now his face was covered in bandages from where the exploding robot head had struck him. His expression bore a kind of desperate madness, and his lips were pulled in a snarl. He said, "That was quite the little scene you orchestrated on my ship, Brandon, though I feel your father had more to do with it than you. Since you thought you were so clever, I thought we might try this little game again but with higher stakes. As you can see, I'm at the Daivik residence. Your father, whom I assume is watching this with you, spared no expense on this luxurious home. I've turned it into something of a base of operations for the time being. Our client is most displeased that you haven't been terminated yet, so they felt it would be appropriate if the deed were done in your parents' home. The rules are similar to last time in that you are expected to turn yourself over, but now I have an additional requirement. Your father must voluntarily resign his position at Assassins Inc. I've grown rather fond of the Vice President title. Oh, and perhaps it goes without saying, but I'll say it anyway... I have your mother, and if you do not comply with my demands I will surely enjoy killing her... Slowly. Bit by bit. I will cut her limb from limb, and I will leave her severed head on your father's desk... See you soon."

The transmission ended.

The sons glanced at one another and then at their father, but no words were shared. After a few moments Brandon finally broke the silence. "So Raxle Naste has to die now, right? I'm assuming that we are all in agreement on that?"

"Without question," Halcard said. "His death throes will stand as a reminder to all of what happens when you fuck with Lynx Rufus's family."

Shivers ran down Akistrodon's spine. There was something about his father's tone that made the hairs on the back of his neck stand. He had only seen his father this angry a few times, and it always ended poorly for whomever instigated it.

Brandon shivered and said, "Alright, so what's the plan? I don't think they'll buy a robot this time."

Halcard nodded. "We are headed for Earth now. As soon as we get there, we are going to send a drone to scope out the house."

"Won't they be able to pick up a drone's signal?" Jack asked.

"Not this drone," Halcard said. "It's a new Vertan prototype. Nothing will be able to see it."

Jack nodded.

"I've hired Lenis to stay with us for the time being. Given the amount of money I've offered, her team is more than willing to risk their necks for us again, and they have already proven they can be trusted."

"What are you thinking?" Brandon asked.

"I don't know yet. We'll see what the situation looks like, and then we'll formulate a plan."

"So do you think Raxle Naste was behind this whole thing from the beginning?" Brandon asked.

"It certainly looks that way," Halcard said. "Only one thing is for certain."

"What's that?"

"Either way, that bastard dies today."

"Holy shit, that's a lot of fire power," Brandon said.

As his father had promised, the drone was able to move in undetected and provided them field data of the house. The only problem was that none of it was good news.

The images from the drone were broadcasted up on the screen. His parents' home was still located in the rural area of Missouri, within the United States, on Earth. When his father had gotten rich in the business, he had purchased several thousand acres of wilderness and had built his wife a sizeable mansion. Typically, the land was beautiful and the house was pristine, but at the moment many of their fields were covered in ships. The area directly around the house was filled with heavy gunnery, tanks, and countless assassins.

"That looks like a military operation," Lenis said. She and a few members of Halcard's trusted staff had joined them in the conference room for this little strategy session.

"Agreed," Halcard said. "Which means that we can't hit them head on. We would never have a chance. I have something else in mind."

"As long as Agkistrodon isn't the one coming up with the plan, I'm happy to listen," Lenis said with a smile.

Halcard nodded. "We are here to get my wife out. That is our top priority."

He glanced around the room making sure that everyone was paying attention before he continued. "Lenis, when I give you the word, I want your team to assault the assassins from the woods to the north. You don't need to fully engage them. I just want you to get their attention. It's a bluff. Pull back into the woods. I want them to send as many of their ground forces into the woods after you as possible. The Warlord will offer you air support."

Lenis nodded. "It can be done. So long as you don't expect me to cause them heavy losses."

"I'm not concerned with taking them out," Halcard said. "I just want you to pull as many away from the house as possible. Make them think we are desperate and trying anything we can."

Lenis nodded. "We can do that."

Halcard nodded. "Good. Naja Ashei, Agkistrodon, and I will be entering the house through a hidden passage. Once we have made it into the house, then I will give you the order to begin engaging the enemy. If all goes well, we can rescue my wife and get out before anyone is the wiser."

"You don't think the enemy has discovered this hidden passage?" Lenis asked.

"No," Halcard said. "I can almost guarantee it."

Brandon smiled beneath his armor. He had only been into his father's secret underground bunker a few times, and he knew it was unlikely that Raxle Naste had found it. No one outside of their direct family knew it was down there, and only Halcard knew all of the secret entrances and exits. When he was building it he hired a contractor to build an impressive labyrinth for him. What the contractors didn't know at the time was that someone had put out a hit on them, so as soon as the job was done, Halcard had killed them and collected the money on their heads. There was literally no one alive that knew the secret entrances but his father.

"This will not be an easy task," Halcard continued. "As I've said, our primary objective is to recover my wife from the house. However our secondary objectives are to find out who put the hit on Brandon and to kill Raxle Naste. If anyone gets a clear shot at Naste, take him out. Don't hesitate. Does everyone understand?"

They all nodded in response.

"Good," Halcard said. "Then let's get started."

CHAPTER NINETEEN

"This passage will lead us to a secret door that comes out behind the dresser in one of the guest bedrooms," Halcard said as he led his sons down the dark cement corridor.

Brandon felt like he was back in the bunker on the trash planet. If he had been told right then to lead them back out he would have been completely lost. He had never truly known just how big his father's secret underground bunker really was. In fact, he had decided not to call it a bunker anymore, because it was more of a secret base.

They had entered through a small cave hidden away in the forest. Once in the cave they had to cut around just the right dark corner, then cut around another corner. At that point they had been facing a rock wall. Halcard had removed a secret panel with a face plate that looked identical to the rock wall. On the panel was a keypad, and he had quickly entered a secret password. As soon as his code was in, the wall slid open revealing a long dark cement passage way.

"What the hell did you build all of this for anyway?" Brandon said. "I mean I get the underground bunker part, but this is a bit much."

"You haven't seen anything," Halcard replied. "There are numerous rooms down here, and they are all filled with supplies for years and years."

"Are you preparing for all-out war?"

"The galaxy is unstable at the best of times," Halcard said. "If an all-out war were to happen, I want us to be prepared. Right about now you ought to be happy I am so paranoid. Now be quiet, we're almost to the house.

Halcard approached a door and flicked on a small screen that showed the room beyond. It was indeed one of the many guest bedrooms, and it appeared to be void of life.

Halcard turned to his sons and said, "Jack, I want you to find your mother. Get her, and bring her back here."

Jack nodded.

Halcard turned to Brandon and continued. "You and I aren't as great at sneaking. While Jack is finding your mother, you and

I will go pay Raxle Naste a visit. His interests are primarily in the two of us, and he may not even know that Naja Ashei is my son yet. We may be able to buy him enough time to sneak her out before Raxle has any idea what's going on."

Brandon nodded.

Halcard said, "This room will put us on the first floor. My office will be just down the hallway. Hopefully Raxle Naste is still there. If not, we will search from room to room. Avoid the atrium if you can."

Brandon and Jack both nodded. The atrium, as his parents called it, was the entryway to the house. If one entered from the front door, they would find themselves in the atrium. It was a large room that kind of served as the central core. There were hallways and doorways that led to every different section of the house. There were two sets of stairs and elevators that went up to the second and third stories. And on both the second and third floor there were long wrap-around balconies. At night the ceiling would be made clear so that they could see the stars, by day it displayed a realistic-looking visual of a night sky. It was the most open spot of the house, and it was obvious why his father wanted to avoid it. Of course one of the doors leading from his large office led right to it, so they would have to be extra quiet.

"Alright my sons," Halcard said. "Just in case anything goes wrong, I want you both to know that I am very proud of you. Now let's find your mother, kill Raxle Naste, and live to talk about it."

They nodded, and Halcard opened his communication channel to Lenis. "We're in the house. Begin the distraction."

As soon as he finished saying this, he pressed a small button and the door slid open silently. As they followed their father into the small room, Brandon turned around and noticed the dresser slide back into its original place. There was no way to tell that it was even a door. Halcard silently showed them how to re-open it just in case.

As they moved toward the door leading out of the room, they heard the gun fire begin outside and knew that Lenis's team was engaged. They could hear a few shouts of orders being given, but none sounded too close. Jack moved up to the door, took out his small, wiry camera, and slid it under the door.

A moment later he determined it was clear and opened the door. He nodded at them once and silently headed to the left. Brandon and his father went right. At the end of the hall was the door to Halcard's office.

They approached slowly and crowded the small door. Halcard nodded at Brandon, and swung open the door. Halcard's armor was too bulky for them to both charge in at the same time, and he led the way, Brandon charging in right behind him.

He had just enough time to see that Raxle Naste was indeed sitting behind his father's desk, then something hit him from behind. It hit him with such force that both he and his father were knocked to the floor.

He tried to roll over, but the weight pressed down on him, and a familiar voice said, "Don't even think about it, Agkistwodon."

"Mr. Gammon," Brandon said, glancing over his shoulder at the hulking frog-like form of his boss. "Good to see you, too."

"Put them on their knees and take their guns," Raxle Naste said from where he sat comfortably in Halcard's chair.

Mr. Gammon and a couple of other assassins pulled Brandon and his father to their knees and disarmed them. Knowing Brandon's fondness for things that go boom, Mr. Gammon took his grenades and proudly hung them from his chest like a medallion. Brandon couldn't help thinking of what a dick his boss was.

Raxle Naste stood up and stepped around the desk. "I've been waiting for this day for a very long time, Lynx Rufus."

"Where's my wife?" Halcard said, his voice even icier than Jack's.

"That's not what you need to concern yourself with at the moment," Raxle Naste said. He rubbed at the bandages on his face. "You've been a huge pain in my ass for far too long, and now your son becomes an equally huge pain. What is it with this family? I have a mind to burn this whole house to the ground."

He paced in front of them, constantly touching the wet bandages on his face. The blood was slowly seeping through, and the wounds hadn't been properly treated. For the first time, Brandon got the impression that Raxle Naste might really be losing his mind.

"You know Raxle," Halcard said, "I spent years trying to groom you into being a good Director, and I tried to forgive the fact that your ambition constantly tried to lead you to find a way to stab me in the back. This time you've gone too far. You put a hit out on my son and threatened my wife... I'm going to kill you."

Raxle Naste laughed. "Lynx you fool, I didn't put the hit out on your son."

"Then who did?"

"Well," Raxle Naste said, "that's just something you'll have to wonder about in the afterlife."

Raxle Naste drew his side arm and shot Halcard directly in the chest. Brandon screamed and struggled to rise, but they held him in place. Halcard went limp beside him and fell over landing on the floor, his helmet facing up.

Brandon snarled at Raxle Naste. "You bastard! I'm going to kill you!"

Raxle Naste laughed and stepped in front of the Brandon. He leaned down so that their faces were close and said, "That's the same empty threat your father just made, and now he's dead. Like father like son I guess."

"Fuck you," Brandon spat, then using everything he had thrust himself forward and slammed his metal helmet against Raxle Naste's bare face. There was a sickening crunch as Naste's nose was shattered. He screamed in pain and rage as the blood started pouring from his nose.

Mr. Gammon and the other assassins tackled Brandon to the ground, and fought to get control of him, but that was all part of his plan. As they pulled him back up to his knees, Naste said, "Now you die, you little…"

He cut himself off when he saw the grenade in Brandon's hand. Brandon had managed to steal one back from Mr. Gammon in the shuffle. Brandon smiled and said, "You can go to hell with me, you son of bitch."

Slowly Naste said, "I don't believe in hell."

"It's an expression!" Brandon said. "What is with you people!? Has no one ever heard of that!?"

The other assassins took a collective step back. Mr. Gammon backed up a little, but kept one hand on Brandon's shoulder. He seemed to be torn between fleeing and trying to manhandle the grenade away.

"What's to keep me from shooting you, and having Mr. Gammon hurl the grenade out of the room?" Naste asked.

"The fact that you don't know what kind of charge I have set on these things. See I'm really quite fond of grenades, and as it was pointed out to me by my recently-deceased best friend, it really is a wonder I've never killed myself with one of these, 'cause I have to admit I do love tampering with the charge timers. For all you know the moment I let of this little button it might blow. Of course you can always ask my direct supervisor. Mr. Gammon has coached me on multiple occasions for my poor grenade safety standards."

"It's twue boss," Mr. Gammon said. "He's not vewy caweful with gwenades. He might not have mowe than a half second chawge."

"I find that highly unlikely. You…"

"Yet you aren't shooting me," Brandon interrupted, "because when it comes right down to it, the great Director Raxle Naste…"

"That's Vice President," Naste corrected.

Brandon ignored him and said, "Director Raxle Naste is a coward. How did my father put it? A creature of opportunity?"

Naste glared at him, but didn't respond. Brandon continued. "I know Naria was the one that came up with the scheme to bring me in. That wasn't even you. I bet this scheme wasn't, either. In fact, my father didn't think you were the one to put up the hit from the beginning, because it was an idea that would have required an intelligence you don't have!"

"Be Silent!" Naste screamed.

"While we're sitting here," Brandon said, "let's have a moment of truth. Do you know that everyone in Assassins Incorporated thinks you're a joke? I don't mean just the bigwigs like my father, but us little peons, too. Every single person in the company laughs about what a back-stabbing little bitch you are. No one, and I mean no one, buys any of the crap you spew."

"Shut up!" he screamed.

"It's a good thing you're so good at kissing ass or you would never have made it as high as you have, because no one respects you in the slightest. Oh, and also, everyone thinks you have a small penis."

"I will kill you!" Naste snarled, white foamy spittle flying from his mouth.

"And still he doesn't pull the trigger," Brandon said. Then turning over his shoulder and looking at Mr. Gammon he added, "And you, you big toad-looking bag of balls, you are the worst boss I've ever had. Seriously, your first name is Garret and your 'R's come out as 'W's. Did your parents hate you? Is that why they gave you that name? And is that why you're such an asshole?"

"I got supewvisow of the month one time!" Gammon cried.

"Probably because whoever voted on it was scared you would hop on them! Or maybe they thought it was a big joke. Yeah that's more likely, because you aren't just an awful boss you're an awful… Toad-person thing. I don't even know what your species is called, and no don't tell me because I don't care. A supervisor is supposed to encourage employees and offer guidance, but all you ever do is act like the biggest dick possible."

"Do you ever shut up!?" screamed Naste, stepping toward him again.

"Yeah, when I'm dead, you wanna see?" he replied as he held his grenade up menacingly.

Naste hurried to move away again, sidestepping toward the fallen Halcard. Suddenly Halcard's foot came up and drilled the back of Naste's knee. There was a loud pop, and before Naste had time to fall Halcard was on him. The two hit the floor in a pile, and Halcard immediately rose over Naste and began hammering heavy gauntlet blows to the man's face.

It took Brandon a moment to assess what was happening. He had thought his dad was as dead, as Raxle Naste did. When his brain caught up he tried to rise, but Mr. Gammon's brain had apparently caught up first. He tackled Brandon to the floor again, and rose over top of him. The sheer weight of Gammon would have shattered his bones if not for his armor. Gammon struggled to get control of him and Brandon said, "Wait! Grenade! It's slipping! One Second charge! Slipping!"

Gammon immediately pulled away, but as he did Brandon grabbed his huge lower frog lip with one hand, and with the other jammed the grenade elbow deep down his huge throat with the other.

Gammon fell away trying to regurgitate the grenade. The other assassins immediately bolted out the room. He had lied about the one second charge, but there wasn't much time. Brandon rolled to his feet, grabbed his dad by the back of the armor, and said, "Grenade! Move!"

Halcard immediately released Raxle Naste and the two of them charged for the nearest door. They dove out, and Brandon turned just in time to see his boss's big toad head explode. The impact knocked the rising Naste back to the ground and showered him in green slime.

"How about that," Brandon said. "Not every day you get to blow up your boss's head. Wonder how that will affect my next evaluation?"

"We've got to move," Halcard ordered, as he rolled to his feet.

"How are you not dead by the way?" Brandon asked.

"New Vertan armor underlay," Halcard replied. "Prototype."

"Of course," Brandon said, then glanced around. They were in the Atrium. Not only were they in the Atrium, but assassins were pouring in from the front door. They both charged for a side hallway as the lasers started zipping around them.

They quickly found that the hallway was blocked off, and headed for a different option. As they approached the next hall-way they found themselves face to face with another group of assassins. An assassin in green armor had his rifle pointed right at Brandon's chest. Before he could fire however, a black form fell from the sky and in a single swift movement removed the assassin's head. The next he slashed across the neck, but more we're coming, and they were pushed back out toward the center.

Halcard looked at Jack and whispered, "You were supposed to be finding your mother."

Jack shrugged. "No luck, so I thought I might come die with you guys."

"Well the more the merrier," Brandon said.

They found themselves pushed into the middle of the Atrium floor of their own family home, completely surrounded by assassins. They stood back to back, a father and his sons, prepared for the inevitable. Brandon reflected that he had been too lucky this entire time, and his only regret was that his family had gotten dragged in the middle of it. He yelled, "Everyone hold on!"

The assassins held back shooting for a moment longer so he said, "Listen, we are fellow employees of the company. We're all on the same team... Sort of. The hit is on me, so kill me, let Lynx Rufus and Naja Ashei go. I mean c'mon, do you really want to be responsible for shooting a VP?"

The assassins faltered, and one guy in red armor said, "Fine, just you it is then."

"If you fire that gun, I will wear your entrails like a necklace," Jack said.

The assassins faltered again, but the guy in red armor said, "Any other day that might seem like more of a threat, but you're pretty outnumbered, Naja Ashei. So I guess it's all of them again."

As they raised their guns again, Brandon looked at his brother and said, "Seriously... What good is your reputation?"

Raxle Naste came limping out of the office. His face was even bloodier, his knee was probably broken, and he was covered in Mr. Gammon's stinky green innards. Brandon had to hand it to him, at least he was a tough bastard. Naste moved over to a pillar and leaned up against it and cried, "Kill them! Kill them all!"

Again the assassins raised their weapons to fire, but another familiar voice from above them said, "Belay that order."

Brandon looked up to second floor balcony and said, "Mom?"

Raxle Naste spit out a wad of blood on the ground and said, "Yes... And the client."

Brandon glanced back up at his mother and said, "What the fuck, Mom?"

"We don't use that language in this home," she said, venom pouring from her lips.

"You put the hit out on me!?"

"And I thought my family was dysfunctional." said the assassin in red armor, then realizing that everyone was looking at him coughed and said, "Sorry."

His mother continued. "Maybe if you answered my calls every once in a while it wouldn't have escalated this far."

"Are you fucking serious!" Brandon screamed, "You put a hit out on me because I don't answer your calls!"

"No," she said sternly. "I put a hit out on you because you were a sneaky little shit and thought you could get away with becoming an assassin without me ever knowing."

Brandon, along with everyone else in the room, just stared at her.

After a moment she said, "You know I don't approve of that life style. I never liked your father doing it. I hated when your brother joined. I'll be damned if I have to spend every night for the rest of my life unable to sleep because everyone in my family is out trying to get themselves killed. I want grandchildren, dammit!"

Again the room remained silent. She continued, "So I decided I would show you just how dangerous being an assassin is, and put a hit out on your head."

"That is the most fucked-up thing I've ever heard," Brandon said. Then turning to his brother and father added, "Guys, back me up here."

They both shook their heads and simultaneously said, "Leave me out of this."

Brandon growled and looked back up at his mother. "So let me get this straight, in an effort to convince me that being an assassin is dangerous, you hired every assassin, mercenary, and bounty hunter in the galaxy to kill me."

"You're damn right!" she said.

"And what would I have learned if I had got killed?"

"Oh please," she waved the notion away. "My men are the best damn assassins in the galaxy. I knew you wouldn't get killed. Besides your father is Vice President, all of these people work for him."

"Unbelievable!" Brandon said. "And at the moment, they are all under crazy pants Raxle Naste's thumb, because when you put a hit out on me, the company decided that Dad couldn't be VP until I was dead. And even though they all hate the bastard, they have to do what he says. You really think I could survive against all of these assassins? That's crazy!"

"In all fairness," Jack said, "he really isn't very good."

"Yeah, see," Brandon said, pointing at Jack.

One of the other assassins in the crowd said, "Yeah isn't he the same assassin that got paid in carrots? I mean…"

The assassin fell silent when her gaze fell upon him.

"Mom, this is the craziest shit you've ever pulled," Brandon said. "And you've pulled some crazy shit."

"I can be crazy if I want," she spat. "I'm your mother! I brought you into this galaxy, and I can take you out!"

"Yeah," he replied. "I'm seeing that."

She glared at him a moment longer, and said, "Promise me that you will quit your job and go to medical school, and I will call off the hit."

"Medical School? Really?"

"Yes," she said, folding her arms across her chest.

"You can't do that!" Raxle Naste screamed. "Men! Kill…"

Before he could finish the statement, Brandon spun, raised his gun, and put a laser bolt straight through Raxle Naste's forehead. He did it fast enough that no one in the room had time to react. As his body slid to the floor, Brandon shrugged and said, "What? I'm a quick draw. Doesn't mean I'm not a shitty assassin. And I told him I was going to kill him, and I kind of had to do that first while it was still legal. Alright, Mom, you've got a deal."

"You promise?" she asked.

"I promise," he moaned.

"Alright," she said. "Then the hit is officially canceled."

Groans went up through the room, and Lynx Rufus stepped forward. "Which means I'm your Vice President again, and I order all of you to clean up that frog mess in my office and then get the hell out of my house. And toss Raxle Naste's corpse in the dumpster on your way out."

The assassins' groans grew louder, but they slowly began shuffling out the door. As they did, Halcard opened a channel on his communicator and said, "Attention all assassins, bounty hunters, and my crew on The Warlord. Cease fire immediately.

The issue has been resolved. It's over."

Brandon slipped to the floor and laid on his back. Staring up at the atrium ceiling he said, "Well it is kind of nice to be home."

Jack looked down at him. "So medical school..."

"Oh shut up," he replied. "If you aren't careful you'll be the next person she puts a hit on. I swear she gets crazier by the day."

"I can still hear you," his mother replied.

"Love you, Mommy," he said.

"Are you boys going to be able to stay for supper?" she asked. "Where's that girlfriend of yours, Brandon? I'm dying to meet her."

"Oh yeah, you guys would probably get along great," he said. "She wants to kill me, too. For your money!"

"Speaking of which," Halcard said, "that is still one matter that we need to address. From a legal stand point she didn't break any laws, so it's not like we can put her in jail or anything."

"Maybe we can pay Lenis to haul that trash off," Jack said. "Lenis is a bounty hunter after all. That's only a step up from garbage collector."

"Hey, you just gave me a great idea," Brandon said. "I know exactly what we can do with her."

CHAPTER TWENTY

"So what now?" Jack asked, as they slowly worked on removing Naria's restraints.

"Well, I guess I have to go to medical school," Brandon said. "Though I'm going to work on convincing Mom that I would be better off doing something else."

"Good luck," Jack said.

"Right," he replied. "She's apparently already started enrolling me. The only really good thing that's come of this is that I talked to Human Resources on the way here, and they agreed to pay out my vacation and sick days along with retirement savings."

"Really?" Jack replied. "That's rare."

"Yeah, they said given the circumstances they felt they could make an exception."

"Strangely nice of them."

"Yeah after all of this, I think the company wants to end on good terms and stay as far away from me as possible," he said, as he worked on removing Naria's mouth restraint. "I mean, I was kind of responsible for killing a ton of employees and damaging a shit load of equipment."

"Actually it was all Mother."

"Very true," he replied, and then gave Naria a glare. "But somehow I've acquired this reputation as someone that really fucks things up. Typical me, I guess."

Jack nodded. "It's better than the carrot thing. I doubt anyone in the company is even talking about that now. Our mother is going to be more feared and renowned than father or I."

Brandon finally removed the restraint from Naria's mouth, and said, "There we go."

She immediately cried, "You can't do this to me! I love you, Brandon! Can't you forgive me!?"

"Wait...Why did we remove the mouth thing again?" Brandon asked.

"You know," his brother said, "I'm not really sure."

They both chuckled.

Naria glared at them. "I can't believe you're doing this to me!

I loved you! I was a good girlfriend!"

"You were," Brandon said. "Right up to the point where you tried to kill me."

They both turned and started walking back onto the ship.

"Please!" she cried. "You can't leave me here like this!"

He glanced back once as the door started to raise. "Oh please, you'll fit right in on this planet."

The door shut firmly, and The Warlord ascended into the sky, once again leaving the trash planet behind.

THE END

ABOUT THE AUTHOR

Phillip Drayer Duncan was born in Eureka Springs, Arkansas and has spent most of his life in the Ozarks. He currently resides in Anderson, Missouri. Along with reading and writing like a madman, his passions include kayakin, canoein, fishin, shootin, video games, and pretty much anything nerd related. Throughout the warm months, he can be spotted on the river, around a campfire, or at a concert. In the cold months, he can be found hermitting amongst a pile of books and video games. His greatest dream in life is to become a Jedi, but since that hasn't happened yet, he focuses on writing. He currently has four novels and ten short stories published.

For more information about Phillip Drayer Duncan and his writing, or to contact him...

PhillipDrayerDuncan.Com

Phillip Drayer Duncan on Facebook

Writer_Phill on Twitter

ABOUT THE COVER ARTIST

Mitchell Bentley has shown his creations from coast to coast and border to border, though mainly throughout the Midwest or plains states—often at General or Literary Science Fiction Conventions. Mitchell has been honored with several guest positions and has won many awards. He currently works on a variety of speculative pieces, commissioned work and publications.

You can view—and purchase—much of his fine artwork at http://www.atomicflystudios.com/.

A Bubba in Time Saves None, Edited by Selina Rosen
A Man, A Plan, (yet lacking) A Canal, Panama, Linda Donahue
Adventures of the Irish Ninja, Selina Rosen
The Alamo and Zombies, Jean Stuntz
All the Marbles, Dusty Rainbolt
Almost Human, Gary Moreau
Ancient Enemy, Lee Killouth
The Anthology From Hell: Humorous Tales From WAY Down Under,
     Edited by Julia S. Mandala
Ard Magister, Laura J. Underwood
Assassins Inc., Phillip Drayer Duncan
Bad City, Selina Rosen & Laura J. Underwood
Bad Lands, Selina Rosen & Laura J. Underwood
Black Rage, Selina Rosen
Blackrose Avenue, Mark Shepherd
The Boat Man, Selina Rosen
Bobby's Troll, John Lance
Bride of Tranquility, Tracy S. Morris
Bruce and Roxanne from Start to Finnish, Rie Sheridan Rose
The Bubba Chronicles, Selina Rosen
Bubba Fables, Sue P. Sinor
Bubbas Of the Apocalypse, Edited by Selina Rosen
The Burden of the Crown, Selina Rosen
Chains of Redemption, Selina Rosen
Checking On Culture, Lee Killough
Chronicles of the Last War, Laura J. Underwood
Dadgum Martians Invade the Lucky Nickel Saloon, Ken Rand
Dark and Stormy Nights, Bradley H. Sinor
Deja Doo, Edited by Selina Rosen
Dracula's Lawyer, Julia S. Mandala
Dragon's Tongue, Laura J. Underwood
The Essence of Stone, Beverly A. Hale
Fairy BrewHaHa at the Lucky Nickel Saloon, Ken Rand
The Fantastikon: Tales of Wonder, Robin Wayne Bailey
Fire & Ice, Selina Rosen
Flush Fiction, Volume I: Stories To Be Read In One Sitting, Edited by
     Selina Rosen
Flush Fiction, Volume II: Twenty Years of Letting it Go!, Edited by
     Selina Rosen
*The Four Bubbas of the Apocalypse: Flatulence, Halitosis, Incest,
     and... Ned,* Edited by Selina Rosen
The Four Redheads: Apocalypse Now!, Linda L. Donahue, Rhonda
     Eudaly, Julia S. Mandala, & Dusty Rainbolt
The Four Redheads of the Apocalypse, Linda L. Donahue, Rhonda
     Eudaly, Julia S. Mandala, & Dusty Rainbolt
The Four Redheads: The Wrath of Satan, Linda L. Donahue,

Rhonda Eudaly, Julia S. Mandala, & Dusty Rainbolt

The Garden In Bloom, Jeffrey Turner

The Geometries of Love: Poetry by Robin Wayne Bailey

The Golems Of Laramie County, Ken Rand

The Green Women, Laura J. Underwood

The Guardians, Lynn Abbey

Hammer Town, Selina Rosen

The Happiness Box, Beverly A. Hale

The Host Series: The Host, Fright Eater, Gang Approval, Selina
    Rosen

Houston, We've Got Bubbas!, Edited by Selina Rosen

How I Spent the Apocolypse, Selina Rosen

I Didn't Quite Make It To Oz, Edited by Selina Rosen

I Should Have Stayed In Oz, Edited by Selina Rosen

In the Shadows, Bradley H. Sinor

International House of Bubbas, Edited by Selina Rosen

It's the Great Bumpkin, Cletus Brown!, Katherine A. Turski

The Killswitch Review, Steven-Elliot Altman & Diane DeKelb-
    Rittenhouse

The Leopard's Daughter, Lee Killough

The Lightning Horse, John Moore

The Logic of Departure, Mark W. Tiedemann

The Long, Cold Walk To Mars, Jeffrey Turner

Marking the Signs and Other Tales Of Mischief, Laura J. Underwood

Material Things, Selina Rosen

Medieval Misfits: Renaissance Rejects, Tracy S. Morris

Mirror Images, Susan Satterfield

Mirror, Mirror and Other Reflections, James K. Burk

More Stories That Won't Make Your Parents Hurl, Edited by Selina
    Rosen

Music for Four Hands, Louis Antonelli & Edward Morris

My Life with Geeks and Freaks, Claudia Christian

The Necronomicrap: A Guide To Your Horooscope, Tim Frayser

Playing With Secrets, Bradley H & Sue P. Sinor

Redheads In Love, Linda L. Donahue, Rhonda Eudaly, Julia S.
    Mandala, & Dusty Rainbolt

Reruns, Selina Rosen

Rock 'n' Roll Universe, Ken Rand

Shadows In Green, Richard Dansky

Stories That Won't Make Your Parents Hurl, Edited by Selina Rosen

Tales from Keltora, Laura J. Underwood

*Tales Of the Lucky Nickel Saloon, Second Ave., Laramie, Wyoming, U
    S of A,* Ken Rand

Tarbox Station, Rhonda Eudaly

Texistani: Indo-Pak Food From A Texas Kitchen, Beverly A. Hale

That's All Folks, J. F. Gonzalez

Through Wyoming Eyes, Ken Rand
Turn Left to Tomorrow, Robin Wayne Bailey
The Twins, Selina Rosen
Wandering Lark, Laura J. Underwood
Wings of Morning, Katharine Eliska Kimbriel
Zombies In Oz and Other Undead Musings, Robin Wayne Bailey

Fantasy Writers Asylum (A YDP Imprint):

Blood Songs
Julia Mandala

Gateway to Corimar
Julia Mandala & Linda L Donahue

Tale of the Black Heart
Linda L. Donahue

Double Dog (A YDP Imprint):

#1:
Of Stars & Shadows,
Mark W. Tiedemann

This Instance Of Me,
Jeffrey Turner

#2:
Gods and Other Children,
Bill D. Allen

Tranquility, Tracy Morris

#3:
Home Is the Hunter,
James K. Burk

Farstep Station,
Lazette Gifford

#4:
Sabre Dance,
Melanie Fletcher

The Lunari Mask,
Laura J. Underwood

#5:
House of Doors,
Julia Mandala

Jaguar Moon,
Linda A. Donahue

Just Cause (A YDP Imprint):

The Bitter End
Selina Rosen

Death Under the Crescent Moon
Dusty Rainbolt

The Ghost Writer
Selina Rosen

It's Not Rocket Science: Spirituality for the Working-Class Soul
Selina Rosen

Meditations of a Hoarder
Melinda LaFevers

Not My Life
Selina Rosen

The Pit
Selina Rosen

Plots and Protagonists: A Reference Guide for Writers
Mel. White

Vanishing Fame
Selina Rosen

Non-YDP titles we distribute:

Chains of Freedom
Chains of Destruction
Jabone's Sword
Queen of Denial
Recycled
Strange Robby
Sword Masters
Selina Rosen

Three Ways to Order:

1. Write us a letter telling us what you want, then send it along with your check or money order (made payable to Yard Dog Press) to: Yard Dog Press, 710 W. Redbud Lane, Alma, AR 72921-7247

2. Use selinarosen@cox.net or lynnstran@cox.net to contact us and place your order. Then send your check or money order to the address above. *This has the advantage of allowing you to check on the availability of short-stock items such as T-shirts and back-issues of Yard Dog Comics.*

3. Contact us as in #1 or #2 above and pay with a credit card or by debit from your checking account. Either give us the credit card information in your letter/Email/phone call, or go to our website and use our shopping carts. If you send us your information, please include your name as it appears on the card, your credit card number, the expiration date, and the 3 or 4-digit security code after your signature on the back (CVV). Please remember that we will include media rate (minimum $3.00) S/H for mailing in the lower 48 states.

Watch our website at
www.yarddogpress.com
for news of upcoming projects
and new titles!!

A Note to Our Readers

We at Yard Dog Press understand that many people buy used books because they simply can't afford new ones. That said, and understanding that not everyone is made of money, we'd like you to know something that you may not have realized. Writers only make money on new books that sell. At the big houses a writer's entire future can hinge on the number of books they sell. While this isn't the case at Yard Dog Press, the honest truth is that when you sell or trade your book or let many people read it, the writer and the publishing house aren't making any money.

As much as we'd all like to believe that we can exist on love and sweet potato pie, the truth is we all need money to buy the things essential to our daily lives. Writers and publishers are no different.

We realize that these "freebies" and cheap books often turn people on to new writers and books that they wouldn't otherwise read. However we hope that you will reconsider selling your copy, and that if you trade it or let your friends borrow it, you also pass on the information that if they really like the author's work they should consider buying one of their books at full price sometime so that the writer can afford to continue to write work that entertains you.

We appreciate all our readers and *depend* upon their support.

Thanks,
The Editorial Staff
Yard Dog Press

PS – Please note that "used" books without covers have, in most cases, been stolen. Neither the author nor the publisher has made any money on these books because they were supposed to be pulped for lack of sales.

Please do not purchase books without covers.

Searching for more protective heroes? Check out the Lumberjacks of High Ridge series here[1]!

And don't miss out on Hallie Bennett updates by joining her VIPs <u>here</u>[2]!

---

1. https://steamyromancereads.com/products/lumberjacks-of-high-ridge-series-e-book-bundle

2. https://www.thearrowedheart.com/hallie-bennett

CHAPTER ONE

TRAVIS GIBSON

"He had no right to touch you."

OWNING A NIGHTCLUB is a real bitch sometimes.

Aside from working odd hours, patrons can be straight-up assholes who assume they're God's gift to humanity and deserve to be treated as such. My staff knows how to handle these kinds of customers—quickly, efficiently, and without drama—so why the hell am I inserting myself into a situation where I don't belong?

Because from the moment I spotted the gorgeous woman draped in blue satin step into The Charleston Cellar, I haven't been able to take my eyes off her.

As the CEO of a conglomerate of upscale lounges around the country, beautiful women frequenting my business aren't an anomaly. Tall, short, thin, round. I've seen them all. Been attracted to many of them. And while at forty years of age I rarely indulged in my attraction to guests, my younger self wasn't as discerning.

So, in theory, this woman shouldn't have caught my attention and held it for the past hour. Nor should a wave of protectiveness have propelled me forward when a man at the bar touched her bare back.

Yet here I am with my hand wrapped around the bastard's wrist, tempted to snap it backward in a painful break if not for the woman's fearful gaze and my bouncer's stern look of reproach.

"Mr. Gibson, I'll take it from here," Jared says, settling a firm hand on the man's shoulder and forcefully guiding him away from the curious crowd watching our altercation.

"You're going to let him get away with that?" An indignant protest rises from the man as he tries to get free of Jared. "He could've broken my wrist!"

"But I didn't. Pity, since it's what you deserve."

Another furious glance back at Jared. "He just threatened me! Do you know who I am? My father is George Hildebrand, and I demand to be released. That maniac should be kicked out, not me!"

Jared and I share a look over the guy's head. There's always a rich prick shouting about his powerful daddy. The sad part is that it's not always college kids either. Grown adults, like this man who looks about my age, use their wealthy parents as a protective shield, too.

"This really isn't necessary." A small hand tentatively tugs on my sleeve, and I face the woman at the center of the debacle. Scarlet flushes the pale skin of her cheeks. Dark pupils eclipse the bright blue of her eyes.

"It is." My hand covers hers and draws it into mine to massage the palm with my thumb. "He had no right to touch you."

Neither do I, but I've never considered myself a 'good' man. It's tough building a business in New York City. Tougher still when you start at the bottom with no connections and even less cash. But I scraped and clawed my way to the top of a luxurious entertainment empire, so now money and connections lay at my feet like sycophants, though an annoying emptiness still gnaws at the edges of my life.

And with each new club I open, it only burrows deeper rather than disappearing. I've become a cliché about the wealthy businessman unsatisfied with his golden lifestyle.

"Didn't we say men would be all over you in that dress?" The woman behind her grins. "You're irresistible, Brooke."

"I agree." The low murmur is only meant for Brooke's ears, and I know she hears me when the tips of her ears turn pink. "Why don't I take you somewhere more private for a breather? Let everyone calm down without having you to focus on."

The crowd of onlookers still hasn't dissipated, and once Brooke notices, her gaze bounces between me and her friend.

"You got some ID on you, big guy?" her friend asks.

Pulling out my wallet, I let the woman snap a picture of my license before she shoos us away. "I'm going to wait for Adeline to get back, then fill her in. You get some fresh air, hon... It'll do you good."

I don't know why Brooke's friend is so gung-ho for us to hang out alone, but I'm not going to question it. She's got my name and address if anything goes sideways, not that I'd ever harm a woman, let alone the curvy one I've had my sights on all evening.

"Um, okay." Brooke shyly peeks up through her lashes, and I use my hold on her hand to tug her behind me through the mass of people dancing and drinking.

With a swift ascent to my office, we're soon locked away in a private cocoon overlooking the club below. Special windows allow us to look down on the crowd without them being able to see us.

Reluctantly, I released her hand and headed toward the bar across from my desk. Maybe a little alcohol will help Brooke relax because right now all I see are nerves radiating from her pores like a bunny running to ground.

"There's nothing to worry about. I don't bite." *Unless asked.* "My name's Travis Gibson, and I own this club. It's my duty to take care of all my guests and see to their comfort and safety."

Perhaps not to this extreme, but she doesn't need to know that.

"Brooke Stanley." She thanks me as I offer her a tumbler of brandy. Her face pinches at the taste, and I bite the inside of my cheek in an effort not to laugh at the adorably innocent reaction.

"So, Brooke Stanley," her name rolls off my tongue, simple and sweet, "what brings you to The Charleston Cellar? Girls' night out?"

Nodding, she licks her lips, immediately drawing my attention to the glistening bow of her mouth. I shift to the side as we both stare out the windows—my cock swelling at the image of her plump lips circling the tip, her eyes holding my gaze as if waiting for approval.

Damn. I swallow the entire glass of expensive liquor with no thought toward savoring it. Brooke on her knees for me would be a hell of a sight.

"We're celebrating my last night in New York."

What? My hand clamps around the empty glass tumbler, the knuckles turning white.

In sixth grade, I got in my first fistfight. Johnny Levinson laughed at the haircut my mom gave me, so I decked him in the jaw. A haphazard brawl broke out between us, and Johnny landed a punch to my gut.

That's how Brooke's declaration feels.

Like the wind has been knocked out of me—my stomach caved in after a brutal blow.

"Oh?" My tone conveys none of my inner turmoil. A skill honed across decades of hiding my true emotions before someone chose to view them as a weakness and take advantage.

Come to think of it, my neutral mask began forming not too long after that fight in sixth grade. Too many bullies found pleasure in making a poor trailer park kid's life hell. Mom was already overworked and running on fumes. Patching my split lips and black eyes only wore her down more.

So, I learned to control myself.

Learned not to react. Outwardly, at least.

It's served me well in life and business.

Brooke nods and sweeps a curl behind her ear. "Adeline and Samantha came to help me with movers and everything before our flight back to Montana tomorrow."

Fucking Montana?

This time I can't stop the grinding of my teeth at her casual announcement.

I may not look like the typical Montanan with my three-piece suits, Aston Martin, and penthouse overlooking

Central Park, but it's where I grew up. Where I began my journey to the top of the corporate world, despite humble beginnings.

"Big Sky Country," I murmur, listing the one detail people tend to remember when they hear Montana. "Is that where you're from originally?"

"Close... Just a little more west. Boise, Idaho. But Guardian Valley will be home now."

I cover a cough of shock with my fist. So much for my legendary control. Brooke shattered it with a well-placed tap of her pink-tipped nail.

Because my business partner and I bought land in Guardian Valley two years ago. An idyllic estate meant to wipe out all the bad memories of my past in that beautiful but godforsaken state.

What are the fucking odds?

CHAPTER TWO

BROOKE STANLEY

"And if you can't flaunt a sexy dress in New York City, where can you wear it?"

"THAT'S QUITE A DISTANCE. New job?" Travis asks as I focus on not passing out from nerves at my current situation—alone with the most attractive man I've ever met.

I'd been grateful when Adeline and Samantha proposed joining me in New York for an impromptu girls' vacation/cross-country move. Their significant others, Heath and Derek, weren't too happy about them gallivanting around New York without protection, but the men were needed on the ranch, and we could handle ourselves.

This past week has honestly been the most fun I've had in the city since moving here eight months ago with my older brother, Ryan, after his transfer to New York's professional hockey team.

Ryan would've helped with moving except the team had a string of away games this week. Besides, all I had to do was direct the movers, not heft furniture out of the condo, down five flights, and into a moving truck.

Ever since our parents died in a freak plane crash when we were six and twelve, I've followed Ryan. When we moved in with our aunt, uncle, and cousins. When he joined a youth hockey league.

I promptly became my big brother's shadow.

Attended every hockey practice. Game. Interview.

He's always been my security blanket. Even now as his social media manager—a role with an expiration date since Ryan's retiring soon. Which means it's time for me to spread my wings and do something of my own, and that's exactly what I plan to accomplish while living in Montana for the next year.

All that's left is to hop on a plane tomorrow and start my new life in Guardian Valley, Montana as a full-time romance author. My dream career after meeting a classmate's author mom at a job fair when I was sixteen.

And what a night of inspiration to kickstart my decision to jump headfirst into writing full-time.

A creepy stranger who felt entitled to more, going so far as to touch me after I refused his advances.

A silver fox dressed in Armani who saved me from said creep with a sexy power move and an air of authority.

It practically writes itself!

"Yes, that's right." It's true I'm starting a new job now that I have the time and resources to devote to it, though that's not the real reason for the move to Montana.

But I can't exactly tell Travis about the inheritance from Mr. Foster, the dead billionaire whose company was responsible for the accident that killed my parents.

It's not something I share with strangers because the looks of pity when they learn about my orphan status make me sick.

I'm also not about to mention the substantial windfall coming my way as long as I live in Guardian Valley for a year, per Mr. Foster's will.

Even if Travis's expensive-looking suit and club owner status negate his need for more money in his bank account.

"Care to elaborate? Or I could guess," Travis muses, his piercing stare traveling down the side of my body in one long sweep.

I shiver under his gaze, feeling exposed.

Vulnerable.

I purchased this dress during a bout of confidence because the satin glided over my plus-size figure in a way that made me feel sexy. A high slit reveals most of my thigh while the practically backless portion—just straps and a band to support my breasts—ends right above my ass.

Frankly, I assumed I'd never wear it out in public. Afraid people would judge my back rolls or the stretch marks on my thigh, but Samantha and Adeline assured me I looked hot before we left the hotel tonight.

And if you can't flaunt a sexy dress in New York City, where *can* you wear it?

Still... I didn't expect a consequence of donning the dress to be hanging out in the club owner's office after he saved me from a pushy groper.

An experienced and attractive man whose mere presence keeps me off-balance.

Which is an unfamiliar feeling since I'm used to plowing through my discomfort most days.

You don't work for a professional athlete like my brother without facing a lot of people and learning to adapt quickly. But

I must have adjusted to the slower Montana life quicker than I thought after my brief visit, because my brain is *not* computing what's happening very well.

"I'm curious what you think I do considering we just met." Am I flirting? Attempting to even though Travis seems way out of my league?

He's older with silver streaking his short hair and trimmed beard, but it's the aura of dominance surrounding him that intimidates me even as it causes my body to heat in sensual curiosity.

"Do I win a prize for guessing correctly?" Travis bares his teeth in a wolfish smile, and my thighs clench together, arousal tingling along my veins.

There's a finer line between lust and nerves than I realized.

"We'll see," I say noncommittally, sipping my drink like the sophisticated woman I'm pretending to be.

He hums in his throat, the low vibrato the closest thing I've ever heard to a growl. *Oh my.* Resting his shoulder on the window, he crosses his ankles, slowly studying me.

"Teacher."

"Nope."

"Librarian."

"Strike two."

Instead of guessing a third profession, Travis straightens and shifts, so his chest brushes my exposed back, pressing me into the window. "How can I trust you're telling the truth?"

I gasped. The intensity of his nearness causes my knees to weaken. A precursor to my whole body dissolving into the hardwood floors beneath me.

"I'm not a liar."

A heated flame sparks where the window reflects his gaze, and he places one hand against the glass above my shoulder, inching forward.

"Because you're a good girl?"

My heart rate doubles at the innuendo, and I swallow hard. "What do you think?"

Suddenly, his nose grazes my neck as he draws it up the column. His lips neatly trace the rapid beat at my throat—the scratch of his beard lighting me up like dynamite.

"I think you're a very good girl who wants to be bad."

"What makes you think so?" Is that my voice? All breathy and sultry?

"Because you're here with me rather than downstairs with your friends. And I can practically smell the desire soaking your cunt right now."

The words are crude, but they're not false. My body slumps more heavily against the window, the cool sensation a relief on my hot skin, my nipples beading at the sensation.

I manage to rally enough sense to whisper, "You still haven't made your third guess."

The deep, masculine chuckle vibrating against my back shouldn't have a direct line to my clit, yet its throbbing need intensifies, and I have to fight not to moan outright.

"Right or wrong, win or lose, I'll be taking a prize."

"And what would that be?" There's a huskiness in my tone that I've never heard before. It's like we're in a dream—two strangers circling each other. A sophisticated man. A curious woman. And there's only one acceptable outcome before we wake up and find ourselves alone again.

"Let's see, shall we? My third and final guess is... social worker."

"Three strikes, you're out." Then I add, "Are all good girls altruistic in your mind? Everything you guessed was a public service position."

"It's part of your charm: feeling the need to serve others."

"But you're wrong about me," I point out.

"Oh, I don't think so. You just like to *serve* in other ways..."

We're entering unfamiliar territory. *Who am I kidding?* This whole conversation feels like a loose puppy I'm desperately trying to catch. I'm flying by the seat of my nonexistent pants here, afraid Travis will realize at any moment that I'm not a skilled seductress.

I'm just a girl who reads way too many romance novels and yearns for her own happily ever after.

A warm palm slides up my leg through the slit of my dress, and it doesn't stop its journey until the heat of Travis's hand cups my bare pussy, stealing the last of my rational thinking.

If I'm leaving New York for good, I'm going out with a bang. *Literally.*

CHAPTER THREE

TRAVIS

"You know what they say... Good girls are bad girls who haven't been caught."

SHE'S TRYING TO KILL me.

First, by announcing a move sending her thousands of miles away from New York, yet somehow near my own property, and second, by traipsing around my club without panties, providing any asshole a potential view of her wet pussy.

And it's definitely *wet*.

My fingers sift through the curls to glide from her clit to her clenching hole, circling the hot flesh before giving in to the urge to slide inside. Nipping the side of her neck, I growl, "You've been wandering around my club like this? Dripping pussy juice, begging for attention?"

In retribution, I pull out far enough to lightly slap her clit, and Brooke arches forward with a high-pitched squeak. "Good girls don't leave their needy cunts exposed for anyone to see."

"You know what they say... Good girls are bad girls who haven't been caught," Brooke teases with a shaky breath.

"Trust me, sweetheart, you're caught." Unable to withstand temptation anymore, I drop to my knees and shove the silky skirt up over her round ass. "It's time to take the reward for my efforts."

"Wh—what are you doing?"

"I can't have my girl returning downstairs slick with need." One of my hands reaches up to rest on her soft lower back, gently guiding her forward so her breasts press firmly against the window while her ass pops out like a beacon.

I'm practically salivating at the sight before me, and I haven't even gotten my mouth on her yet.

"I'm going to clean you up with my tongue, and you're going to come like a good girl with all those people below none the wiser."

"What if someone sees us?" Anticipation rings in her voice, overshadowing the hesitant edge of fear. Her body trembles beneath my hands, and I know it's because the threat of being seen is turning her on even more.

Bad girl, indeed.

I could comfort her by explaining how the windows only work one way—looking out—but why dampen her heightened arousal?

"You mean, what if someone discovers me on my knees fucking your little pussy with my tongue?" Her breath hitches as I kiss down one fleshy cheek until my face is nestled between her glistening folds.

Fuck, she smells good.

"Y... yes." The word is breathed more than spoken as Brooke melts into my embrace.

"Then they'll know what a bad girl you are," I taunt, then dive into my prize.

The first taste is spicy-sweet.

The second, addictive.

And by the third swipe of my tongue through her cunt, I know I'm never letting this woman go. She's mine. It's that fucking simple.

I flick and circle—nip and suck—her swollen clit as my fingers rock inside her, teasing the sensitive spot that makes her jump each time I graze it.

"That's right, sweetheart. Ride my face. Stick that plump ass out and smother me with your dripping hot pussy."

Brooke moans and does as I say, allowing more of her weight to lean on me, and I fucking love it. I could die just like this and be happy that it was eating out my girl that did me in.

Forty years of blood, sweat, and tears to build a kingdom of gold crushed to dust by one woman and her delicious pussy.

A faint knocking tickles the back of my mind, but I ignore it. Brooke is swaying her hips, rubbing her slick cream all over my beard, and I'm not about to stop her pleasure for a fucking visitor.

"Travis... Oh my—" A splash of her orgasm lands on my tongue, and I eagerly swallow, grunting in satisfaction as Brooke shudders above me. Gently, I ease her down from the high until the last wave of her climax rolls through and she's slumped back against my chest.

"Mmm... You were very naughty, sweetheart." And good or bad, she's definitely *my* girl.

Another knock bangs on the door as I nuzzle her neck, sweaty strands of her hair sticking to the soft flesh.

"You should answer them. It sounds important."

"I don't want to. I'm not done with you yet." *Spoiler alert, I won't ever be done.* But I can't exactly drop that bit of news on her. Not when she can so easily be scared off.

Even I'm unnerved by the power of my need to possess her. I've never felt anything like it before.

Guess there's still a part of that poor kid left inside me. The one desperate to have something of his own. Because all the money and clubs don't matter if I don't have my own woman to share them with.

Brooke eases out of my embrace after another knock on the door. "I don't think they're going to leave until you answer them. Why don't I go check in with my friends while you deal with your business stuff? I promise I'll be back." A shy smile flashes my way as she gestures toward the door, where someone's about to receive the brunt of my anger for interrupting us.

I don't like the idea of letting her out of my sight, but she's halfway across the room before I can stop her.

Jaw clenching as she sidles by Jared, who's blocking the doorway, I tell myself it'll only be ten minutes. Tops. Then Brooke will be back in my arms.

Ten minutes.

ONE WEEK LATER

Craggy mountains and green forests are a welcome change from New York's urban jungle. After a seven-hour flight, my jet lands on the private airstrip Braden and I built to access our property easier, and I'm eager to find my errant woman.

Brooke skipped out on me after promising to come back to my office. Rather than keeping her word, she disappeared instead.

Braden: *Good luck finding your mystery woman. Are you sure she's worth the trouble? She did dump your ass without a backward glance.*

I read the text before telling him to *fuck off*. Braden Vanderhorn can be a dick, but when we met fifteen years ago, our plans for the future clicked together perfectly. He wanted to elevate his family's chain of hotels, and I envisioned an international brand of luxurious lounges meant to cater to the world's elite—since those were the people I wanted to learn from.

The years since we became friends and business partners have been full of success with little downtime, so when Braden mentioned purchasing property for group getaways and office retreats, I immediately suggested Montana.

I liked the idea of returning to my home state a wealthy success, prepared to shove it in anyone's face who doubted me.

Of course, that was an angry boy's dream, not a man's purpose, so rather than settling in my hometown of Livingston, we chose Guardian Valley. Its quaint history and charming community is the ideal place to relax and recharge.

Or fuck like rabbits, I muse, imagining all the ways I'm going to punish Brooke for leaving me. Spank her juicy ass then fuck her. Tie her to the bed then fuck her.

Basically, everything comes back to me pummeling that tight pussy of hers hard enough that she knows never to disappear on me again.

If Braden knew my thoughts, he'd probably be less smartass and more concerned over the obsessed stalker vibes I'm giving off.

But my secret's safe for now, and no one's going to stop me from claiming what's mine: Brooke Anne Stanley.

CHAPTER FOUR

BROOKE

"This man is cloaked in rugged dominance..."

THE BLANK WHITE SCREEN mocks me. I've been staring at it for the past hour with no luck, the cursor blinking incessantly as words refuse to write themselves.

"Come on, Brooke," I mutter to myself, lightly tapping my nails along the keys, searching for inspiration.

Okay, so that's not entirely true. I have inspiration. My dreams for the past week have been chock full of inspiration. The hot and sweaty kind. With Travis Gibson starring in all of them.

Maybe that's my problem.

I'm too focused on what might have been with the commanding club owner. After an amazing orgasm, I'd fully intended to return to his office for more sexy times, but Adeline hadn't been feeling well. And at almost six months pregnant, Samantha and I weren't going to let her stay in the lounge when she needed to rest.

Especially with the protective warnings from Samantha's brother/Adeline's husband, Heath, echoing in our heads. Addie's pregnancy had been one of the major reasons he'd been hesitant to let her travel.

So, rather than a memorable night with a silver fox, I spent the evening fetching Addie saltines and water. My New York affair cut short.

Same with my creativity.

Because all of my thoughts were consumed with Travis and possibilities rather than plotting and writing my first romance novel.

Slamming the laptop closed, I get up and wander to the front windows overlooking Serenity Ranch. Mountains rise above the clouds in the distance while trees dot the landscape. A couple of horses graze in a large paddock, and the quiet calm should be relaxing.

But restlessness itches under my skin.

Directionless energy that I have no clue what to do with.

Writing isn't happening at the moment, but there are still a couple of boxes to unpack in the guest room of the cabin I'm staying in. Or I could go on a walk around the property and visit the main house to see if Addie or Samantha want to join me.

But none of that feels right.

Movement in my peripheral catches my eye as a huge chestnut horse trots up the long drive. A cowboy hat obscures its rider's face while a thick shearling coat broadens the man's already wide shoulders.

He looks dressed for winter, even though it's April, but that's Montana weather for you.

The stranger stops at the main house, and I turn away, uninterested in whatever rancher business he has with Heath, the ranch's manager and co-owner with Addie. But it's not even five minutes later when there's a knock at my door.

Maybe Addie or Samantha left the house to give Heath and the stranger privacy?

"Hey, what's—" The greeting stalls in my throat because it's not Samantha or Addie at my door.

No, it's Derek and *Travis freaking Gibson*. Except he doesn't look like the suave man I met at The Charleston Cellar. That man wore tailored suits and bespoke watches. Exuded sharp authority with a snap of his fingers.

But *this* man.

This man is cloaked in rugged dominance—the rougher, wilder counterpart to Travis's appearance in New York. His beard is a little thicker. His eyes are a little harder.

Surely, this isn't who I saw riding up the drive.

"Sorry to bother you, Brooke, but this man says he knows you. I asked him to wait at the main house while I talked with you first, but he wouldn't listen." Derek glares at Travis. The men are comparable in size and Derek's a military veteran, yet there's an edge to Travis that makes me wonder if he couldn't defeat Derek's Army training.

"It's alright. He's a... friend from New York." I wasn't about to announce the truth that this was my *almost one-night stand*. No way would Derek leave then.

I don't know the man too well yet, but from what I've gleaned after numerous meals together, he's protective of those he considers his own and he's not afraid to put himself between a problem and those he cares for.

Like Samantha and her ex-boyfriend.

When she'd relayed the story about how she and Derek got together, I didn't blame her for falling for the gruff veteran. His scars—sustained from the same plane crash that killed our parents—had held him in chains for most of his life. Kept him guarded.

Until his arrival at Guardian Valley and meeting Samantha.

"Are you sure?" Derek asks, placing himself between me and Travis and staring down at me with kind eyes.

"Yes, it's fine. Just ask Samantha. She knows Travis, too."

He hesitates another minute before sighing. "Okay, but I'll be at the paddock if you need anything."

Once he's gone, I invite Travis inside, a maelstrom of emotions whipping through me. "What are you doing here? How did you find me?" Those were my most pressing questions because I'm struggling to understand what's happening right now.

I met Travis, a sophisticated businessman, in New York City.

And now, Travis the unpolished cowboy is here in Guardian Valley, Montana?

"It wasn't too difficult," he says, shrugging out of his coat and tossing it aside. "Guardian Valley is a small town, so new arrivals are a big deal. Especially when they're part of a unique inheritance situation."

"You've been asking about me?" Gossip around here is no joke if townspeople already know who I am. I haven't even been here for a month.

"Of course..." His long fingers roll up the sleeves of his twill button-down, and the reveal of strong, tan forearms draws my attention. The way the muscles tense and flex.

God, I'm getting turned on by his freaking forearms!

"You broke your promise, Brooke." He stalked forward.

"I—I did?"

"You promised to return to me, but you didn't." His finger drifts down my cheek. "What do you think your punishment should be?"

Oh, damn.

"Whatever you deem appropriate," I choke out behind the desire clogging my throat. Desire *and* nerves. I've never been *punished* by a man before. It's a foreign concept, but what I've read in books has been hot.

And my body agrees, if the immediate tingling response between my thighs is anything to go by.

"Wise decision." His hands fall to my hips and slowly turn me to face the back of my couch. "Put your hands here and hold on. Don't," his teeth nip at my ear, "let go. Understand?"

"Yes." My nails dig into the buttery leather as I wait for his next move. Five minutes ago, I was stumped with how to spend the day, and then Travis magically appeared.

After a week of unfulfilling sex dreams, I'm ready for the real thing. I don't care how quickly it's happening. I just need Travis.

"I seem to recall having you in a similar position before. Unfortunately for you, only good girls get fucked with my tongue first. And you've proven to be very, *very* bad by disappearing on me." Travis's warm palm wraps around the front of my throat to tilt my chin up. "Which means, instead of my tongue, you get my cock."

Doesn't seem like too bad of a trade.

Definitely not a punishment.

I hear the rustling of his belt and zipper before his hands find the waistband of my leggings and tug them down with my panties. Cool air brushes my ass followed by a firm slap of Travis's palm on my left butt cheek.

Holy hell! There's the punishment.

He repeats the action on the right side before slipping his fingers lower, two of them thrusting in and out of my already-soaked pussy until his thick cock replaces them a moment later.

"Travis!" I yelp at the sudden intrusion. It's not painful, just unexpected, despite his warning.

"That's right. Scream my name, baby," he grunts in my ear. His hand drops to my breast and squeezes, the flesh overflowing his large palm. "I can't get enough of your pussy. And this ass."

His fingers lightly pinch my backside. "Watching it jiggle and bounce while I fuck you makes me hard as hell."

It occurs to me that Travis really is an ass man because we were in this exact position at his club, too. His broad, muscular body caging mine against the windows, and now the couch.

Tap, tap, tap.

Like an annoying insect, the sound continues as Travis obliterates every fantasy I had this week. The reality of his dominant lovemaking is so much better than what I dreamed up based on books and movies rather than firsthand experience.

Tap, tap, tap.

A sense of déjà vu pops my euphoric bubble because once again someone is interrupting us with a knock on my front door.

"Do. Not. Fucking. Answer." Travis slams his hips forward, and I desperately grab onto the couch cushions in front of me for purchase.

His pace strengthens—driving harder, deeper—until one more stroke of his cock sends me over the edge. I muffle a shout of pleasure, but Travis has no such compunction. He announces his climax with a roar of my name before collapsing against my back.

Tap, tap, tap.

"Goddammit! What is with people screwing up our time together?"

A giggle burst out of me. It *is* kind of sucky timing.

"You're a hot commodity. I guarantee whoever is on the other side of that door is here because of you, just like last time," I say, then call out, "Just a minute!"

Swiftly, I clean up with a couple of tissues and grab my leggings, hopping on one foot then the other before rushing to the door. Travis is as cool as ever, calmly straightening his shirt, and I realize he fucked me fully clothed.

One of these days we need to make it to a bed...

Samantha stands red-faced on the small cabin stoop when I swing the door open.

"Hey..." she waves awkwardly. "Derek said Travis was here, but we had to see it to believe it. Until we heard how *here* he actually was," Samantha whispers with a grin. "Addie went scrambling back to the main house after that."

Oh, god... I can only imagine poor Addie's reaction to what she heard.

"Welcome to Montana, Travis!" Samantha peers around me and smiles even wider. "I came to get you guys for dinner. We're having spaghetti and meatballs tonight."

A group dinner sounds like a terrible idea considering Travis and I still need to talk alone, but my stomach growls right as I prepare to say something.

A frown tugs at Travis's mouth—a mouth that had just been promising sexual punishments—and he nods. "Sounds good. Brooke needs to eat."

Said no one ever.

I'm a big girl. I don't look like I miss meals.

But it's nice to hear Travis encourage me to eat. Clearly, my size doesn't deter him in the least.

What was your first clue? Him eating you out at his club that first night? Or bending you over the couch and fucking you from behind just now?

CHAPTER FIVE

TRAVIS

"A moonlit ride across the Montana wilderness..."

DINNER AT SERENITY Ranch is an interesting affair. Three of the heirs to Dell Foster's billions have arrived for their contractually obligated year in Guardian Valley, and they are as different as can be.

Addie wears thick cardigans and doesn't say much at the table as the bowl of garlic bread is passed around.

Derek is covered in scars and keeps a sharp eye on me like I'm going to kidnap Brooke at any moment. *Okay, so maybe his concern isn't completely unfounded.*

And then there's my girl. She's somewhere in the middle, not as shy as Addie and not nearly as cautious as Derek.

"I've heard the story in town about the heirs of Guardian Valley. Do you know who the rest of the heirs are?"

Addie nods and offers a shy smile. "Yes, thanks to Brooke. She was the missing puzzle piece."

"Oh?"

"My brother Ryan is one, obviously, because we both lost our parents. And the last heir is Hope. We became friends during the trial that ultimately didn't do anything but shove us into the spotlight more," Brooke says, shrugging her shoulders. "We've been friends ever since."

I honed into the details about their failed trial. How could five kids lose their parents in a horrific plane crash and not win? Especially when one of the kids was actually on the plane and suffered lasting scars?

"Foster's lawyers found a loophole absolving them of responsibility," Derek explains after I ask the question weighing on my mind. "The company didn't even cover my skin surgeries. Said I shouldn't have been on the plane in the first place, despite my dad getting prior permission, so I could watch his keynote speech. Somehow *that* particular correspondence was never found. Bastards."

Samantha's palm moves to his back and rubs soothing circles across the man's tense muscles. It's obvious the topic is a difficult one.

"I'm sorry for bringing it up. I understand how some people can be real assholes."

My childhood was full of them.

Livingston is full of them.

I tried talking my mom into moving. To New York. To Guardian Valley. But she refused. It was her hometown, and she wasn't going to let a couple of judgmental jerks run her out of it. Which is admirable, I suppose, but I wish she'd shake off the dust of that old town and move on like me.

Thankfully, the dinner conversation lightens up as we move on to discussing details about Guardian Valley, like the upcoming May Day Parade.

And afterwards, I consider my options for the night. We can retreat to Brooke's cabin, or I can come clean about the other reason it was so easy to find her.

And get away from any more interruptions.

Not wanting secrets between us, I grab Brooke's hand and pull her to a stop outside. "Can I show you something?"

"Now?" Confusion wrinkles her nose as she searches the surrounding area for what I could possibly want to show her.

"If that's okay. I promise it'll be worth it."

Hesitation weighs in the air but eventually Brooke agrees with a nod of her head, so I redirect us to the barn where Derek had me stable my horse, Tenor. It doesn't take long for me to saddle him for a ride back to my place, and the whole time Brooke stares wide-eyed, occasionally asking me questions.

"A moonlit ride across the Montana wilderness isn't exactly what I thought you had in mind."

I chuckle and hug her closer to me, making sure she's secure in my arms after we mount up. "Didn't fit your idea of the New York club owner?"

"Not exactly... Although, you pretty much demolished my first impression after showing up on my doorstep in full cowboy regalia," she says. "Not that I'm complaining."

My chin rests on the side of her head as Tenor carefully walks back to Gibson-Vee Ranch, the name Braden and I settled on after much debate. Rather than cutting through Harper's Landing, I decided to take the longer and technically legal route of following the road back home.

Our breath fogs the air as millions of stars shimmer above us. It's a beautiful, cool night for an evening ride.

"I'm a man of many talents," I joke. "In this business, it pays to be flexible. Adaptable. So, when a situation calls for the sharp businessman, I slip into my three-piece suits and take extra time on my appearance. When I'm in Guardian Valley, where jeans and boots are the norm, I get to dress more casually. But they're both me."

"What are you doing in Guardian Valley, though? It's difficult to believe you bought a new wardrobe and a horse all to find me."

"That's the surprise." We slowly enter Gibson-Vee land and halt in front of my two-story house. Braden's is built a little further down the paved driveway. "Welcome to my home."

CHAPTER SIX

BROOKE

"That's all fate."

SHOCK STRAIGHTENS MY spine as I stare at the gorgeous mansion in front of me. "Your home?" Surely, I couldn't have heard him correctly.

"Yep, and how you're feeling right now is how I felt when you first mentioned Guardian Valley at the club," he says, guiding us toward the stables—an obviously newer structure than what Serenity Ranch has.

Surprisingly, there's a man waiting to greet us and take Tenor. He dips his head in greeting then takes the reins once we dismount.

Travis has staff. Like round the clock *staff*?

"Come on, I'll give you a tour of the house and explain things more. Although there's really not a logical explanation for both of us just happening to live in Guardian Valley. That's all fate."

The home is cozy with oversized furniture and a warm color palette. I imagine the reds and oranges play well in the daylight against the green and blue backdrop of sky and mountains outside. A view on full display through the massive floor to ceiling windows. Whoever designed this place was clearly a professional with great taste.

"I grew up in Montana. A town called Livingston that's two hours away. My mom raised me by herself, so money was tight," Travis begins, holding my hand as we walk through room after gorgeous room. "Kids bullied me for living in the trailer park. For wearing donated clothing. You name it, and I got teased for it. Until I started defending myself. That's when the fighting started."

He says it so nonchalantly like it doesn't matter now, but it's obvious his childhood shaped him into the man he is today.

"Busted lips, black eyes. Those were my reality until I finally got smart. Stopped adding more stress to my mom's life. I learned to control my emotions, my reactions to the taunting. Self-control has served me well from the moment I graduated high school to building my company."

That explains how easily he slips from passionate lover to collected businessman around others. Even earlier when Samantha got us for dinner, I'd still been fighting to catch my breath and bottle up the raging desire coursing through my blood, but Travis acted like she hadn't just heard him shout his pleasure not ten feet away.

"Now it makes sense... Why you react so calmly in the face of interruptions. Publicly at least," I amend, recalling his annoyance when our sexy times were cut short.

"Fuck interruptions. The point is all those years of honing my control are shot. Because *you* unravel me." His arms circle my waist and tug me into his chest. "I saw you then almost broke that asshole's wrist. I stole you away to my office to bury my face in your pussy not five minutes later. Hell, I flew the private jet here to claim you as mine permanently. My control is in tatters when it comes to you."

Whoa. I'm struggling to understand how I'm the woman holding this much power over Travis. He could literally have anyone. Anyone he's known for more than mere hours, yet I'm the one he wants. The one he can't get out of his mind.

It's heady stuff.

I've had a couple of boyfriends in the past, but they never made me feel like this. Valuable. Necessary. Sexy as hell.

I'm just a run of the mill girl with big dreams. Who am I to inspire such passion? Except Travis sees me as more.

And makes me believe he's right, trumping my self-doubt. I mean, the man flew his private jet across the country to find me. That's one heck of a booty call if this wasn't more to him.

If *I* didn't mean more to him.

"Does this mansion have a master suite? A bed? Because I think it's time you lost control somewhere I can fully enjoy it," I taunt, embracing this boost of confidence created by his admission.

A slow grin spreads across Travis's handsome face. "Oh, sweetheart, you have no idea what you've just unleashed."

It's a warning, but all I feel is anticipation.

A second later, he tosses me over his shoulder. Literally. My belly to his shoulder. My face staring—*and admiring*—his firm ass beneath those Wranglers as his palm squeezes my hip.

It feels like that scene from Grey's Anatomy when Alex and Jo finally have sex and he carries her upstairs, except I never thought something like that could happen to me because I'm not a thin Tinkerbell look alike.

Turns out that doesn't matter as long as you have a man strong and determined enough to whisk you away to his bed.

And just like Jo from the show, I'm internally squealing in excitement over what comes next.

Complete freedom in bed with Travis—no distractions or interruptions in sight.

Yes, finally!

The journey to the home's master suite passes in a blur of tasteful decor and jean-clad legs before Travis lowers my feet to the hardwood flooring of his room. His hands drop to the belt at his waist, slowly unbuckling the leather before drawing it through the denim loops.

Why is that so sexy?

I catalog his every move from the metal clank of his belt hitting the floor to the whisper of his zipper sliding downward. The denim loosens around his waist, allowing Travis to free the hard bulge of his arousal from its restraints after shoving the jeans and boxer briefs out of his way.

"Is this where I get to *serve you in other ways*?" I recall his smug assumption from the first night we met—before I distracted him with the discovery of my panty-less pussy.

Travis grins, fond remembrance flaring in his dark eyes. "Clever girl." He sits on the bed and motions me closer. A slight tug on my sweatshirt lets me know what he wants—me on my knees for him.

Complying, I kneel before him, bracing my hands on his thighs. Travis palms his hard cock before offering it to me, lowering the glistening head until it taps my bottom lip. "Open up, sweetheart. It's time to show your man how well you suck his cock."

My man.

I like the sound of that.

His low command beckons me closer, and we both groan as my mouth wraps around the tip of his cock with gentle suction. Both of Travis's hands dive into my hair—whether to guide my motions or provide stability, I'm not sure, but the feel of his fingertips scratching at my scalp has me swallowing more of his hot length, eager to please.

"Fuck, Brooke... Just like that..."

His murmured praise lulls me into a dreamlike haze as a push-pull rhythm forms between us. It's controlled like Travis. Not brutal or punishing. But the longer time stretches, the more of a wild edge seeps into his body, tension outlining his muscles as I attempt to shatter it.

"So perfect..." A moment later, Travis grunts before the salty warmth of his release fills my mouth, and he massages my scalp, stroking my hair. "You're so beautiful... My sweet Brooke..."

I've barely caught my breath when I'm hauled into his arms and rolled beneath his muscular body. He tenderly kisses my lips before rearing back with a determined expression. "Now, it's your turn."

The rest of our clothing quickly disappears as Travis tosses the offending items to the floor. It's my first time seeing all of his tan skin and supple muscles on display. And what a sight. Where I'm all soft curves—some might say *too* many curves—Travis is the opposite. Hard ridges form shadows along his abdomen. Wiry hair covers his chest before trailing downward.

My hand reaches out to follow the path except Travis traps my hand against the mattress as his tongue licks across my skin.

Neck. Breasts. Belly. Until his heavy breaths warm my pussy, his face burrowing between my thighs.

The first flick of his tongue sends my back bowing up from the bed.

The second has my legs trying to snap together to keep him in place—an impossible feat with his broad shoulders holding me wide open.

And by the third, I'm embarrassingly close to coming already, the sensuality of sucking his cock combined with Travis's talented mouth shooting me straight into the sky like a Fourth of July firework.

"Travis!" Stars burst behind my eyelids as I fight to catch my breath. Another impossible endeavor because he wastes no time plunging his cock deep into my still-pulsing channel.

"I'm right here, sweetheart. You've been such a good girl. Swallowing my cock. Coming on my tongue. Give me one more of your sweet releases, then I'll let you rest."

A wayward thought towards needing to build my stamina flashes in my mind before it's swiftly forgotten in the wake of Travis's rough thrusts burying hard and fast into my pussy, shoving me higher up the mattress with each powerful snap of his hips.

"Please... I'm not sure I can..." Multiple orgasms aren't a stranger to me, at least when they come by my own hand. But this is way different than battery-operated climaxes.

This is a hundred times more intense.

And it's scary as hell.

"You can," Travis growls, bending low to whisper in my ear, "Trust me, sweetheart. Give me what I want and let go."

Like his voice has a direct line to my clit, my body obeys, and I cling to Travis, my nails digging into his shoulders as we both fly into the sun—two lovers melded together as one.

CHAPTER SEVEN

TRAVIS

"There's a gnashing, feral part of me that wants to force the man away from Brooke..."

BROOKE AND I SPEND the weekend together at my place after her sexual challenge, taking full advantage of being alone and having a king-sized bed to roll around on. The sex is amazing, but what's even better is hanging out with Brooke. Exchanging stories about our pasts and hopes for the future.

"You promise you don't think it's a silly dream?" she asks after admitting her desire to be a full-time romance author.

It's Monday morning, and we're at her cabin for fresh clothing and to collect her laptop after I drove us back to Serenity Ranch. Frankly, I'd be happy if she remained in my tees and sweats for the foreseeable future, but even I know—in my crazy, obsessive brain—that's a ridiculous demand.

"Hell no. Romance is a billion-dollar industry. Why would it be silly to be a part of it? If writing about love is something you enjoy, then it sounds like a wise business decision."

Her shoulders slump in relief as a tremulous smile follows my assertion. "That's if I'm any good. I haven't published anything yet."

I sling her quilted duffel bag over my shoulder once it's zipped closed with a few outfit changes and toiletries. We didn't discuss how long she'd stay with me or when I'd need to return to New York City, but the weight of what she packed was reassuring. Means this is more to her than a weekend fling.

Not that I'd let her get away with that type of thinking.

I tried my damnedest over the weekend to prove how much she means to me through a marathon of orgasms and being more vulnerable than I've ever been with anyone else.

"Stop doubting yourself before you've even begun," I say, pulling her in for a side hug after she locks up the cabin and we head toward her car.

"What the hell are you doing here, Gibson?" A man yells across the open expanse between the main house and Brooke's cabin. Immediately, my arm moves protectively over Brooke as I guide her behind me.

I recognize Heath and Derek's tall forms leaping from the house porch, hurrying to catch up to the angry man currently bearing down on us.

Samuel Winters—the owner of Harper's Landing and neighbor to Gibson-Vee Ranch.

Looks like he's still pissed about our offer to buy his land, despite it being extremely generous and meant to help his struggling family business.

"Winters." My voice remains calm and neutral. However, there's a gnashing, feral part of me that wants to force the man away from Brooke to ensure her safety.

Not that I think Winters is dangerous, but when a man has fury fueling his steps, there's no telling what he might do in the heat of the moment.

"*Winters*," he sneers, mocking my cool tone. "You've got some nerve showing up here. Think you can steal another ranch for your playboy playground?"

"What's he talking about?" The quiet question comes from behind, where Brooke is trying to outmaneuver me to see what's going on.

Not gonna happen.

"No one is stealing anyone's ranch. If you're going to accuse me of something, Winters, at least make it believable." I force a note of boredom into my tone. "Braden and I offered an extremely lucrative deal—one, according to public records, that would be a godsend—and you turned it down. End of story."

"Except it isn't. Because you and Vanderhorn keep hounding me to sign a new deal. Refusing to take no for an answer." Winters huffs and clenches his fists at his sides. My gaze drops to the potential threat before rising again.

"I don't know what you're talking about. Another offer hasn't been made."

"Tell that to the twenty-page contract in my paper shredder."

Winters may be brash, but I've never taken him for a liar. Which means Braden has some explaining to do. Why would he approach Winters again, knowing the man's adamant refusal to sell?

Some clients hemmed and hawed. Were stubborn holdouts hoping to drive up prices. They expected to be wooed with bigger and grander deals. Winters did *not* fit that profile.

He has an emotional connection to the land. It's his family's legacy. Money won't sway him, and Braden should know that.

"Again, I have no clue what the hell you're talking about, but you can be sure I'll be talking with Braden. If this is his doing, then I'll make sure he stops bothering you."

"See that he does," Winters growls as Heath puts a hand on his shoulder, attempting to calm his friend down.

Snagging Brooke's hand, I usher her to her car while keeping a watchful eye on Winters. "If you'll excuse us, we have somewhere to be. I'll talk to Braden and clear up any misunderstandings," I say by way of farewell.

Derek, Heath, and Winters remain silent, though their glares could burn a hole through the ozone, let alone my back.

So much for the goodwill I might have earned during dinner. Seems Winters ground it out with the heel of his weathered boots.

Good thing I'm used to being an outcast.

Because I don't give a fuck what those men think of me. The only opinion that matters is Brooke's.

CHAPTER EIGHT

BROOKE

"From the moment I first saw you in my club, it was game over for me."

"THAT WAS INTENSE."

Travis and I are finally back at his place after the showdown with Samuel. I've only met the man once before when he had Sunday supper with everyone at Serenity Ranch, but I didn't peg him for a quick temper.

"I'm sorry you had to see that. I don't know what Braden was thinking if this is his fault." Travis sets my overnight bag on his dresser before wrapping his arms around my waist and pulling me in for a hug.

I squeeze him tight and bury my head in his chest, his heartbeat a steady rhythm against my cheek. "Either way, you didn't deserve to be ambushed. Though you handled it like a champ." I press a kiss to his sternum and smile up at him. "That cool demeanor of yours came in clutch today."

"Told you it serves me well. Around everyone but you, of course." His lips brush over my forehead. "You snap my control as easily as a stray twig. From the moment I first saw you in my club, it was game over for me."

"I should send a thank you note to whoever designed that dress."

Travis chuckles as he slowly walks us back toward his bed. "It wasn't just the dress, sweetheart. It was you. For decades, I've been alone. Content with building my business so my mom and I would never know the struggle of my youth again."

When the back of my knees hit the mattress, we stop, and he cups my face with both of his hands. The large palms are gentle and tender as he strokes the delicate skin with his fingertips.

"But something's been missing, and I couldn't figure out what it was until you appeared. Sexy and sweet and damn irresistible. I knew you belonged to me before I even knew your name. A gift just for me."

The declaration is firm, confident—full of promise and forever.

"Travis..." Words fail to materialize. What do you say when the man of your dreams bares his soul to you?

Reciprocate the vulnerability.

Shoving aside the ball of nerves rattling around my stomach, I inhale a deep breath and then release it.

"Ever since my parents died, my brother has been my security blanket. I've followed him around the country while he pursued his dreams, too afraid to venture off by myself." My eyes drop from his for a brief moment. It's embarrassing to admit how much of a coward I've been. "Until now. Before we learned of the inheritance, I decided this year would be different. I'd leap into writing. Move out on my own. So many huge changes. Then I met you—the biggest surprise of them all."

"But a good one?" he asks.

"The best." I bite my lip as my anxiety heightens. This is where I lay it on the line for him. Just like he did for me. And even if I think I know his response, there's still a niggling fear in my heart that this is all just temporary.

A whirlwind fling before Travis jets back to the city.

"You bring out this spontaneous side of me. Make me feel comfortable while also full of butterflies. But all of this scares me, too, because what if I'm not enough?"

"What are you talking about? You're more than enough." Travis steals a hard kiss that leaves me breathless, clutching at his shoulders.

Swallowing past the lump in my throat, I soldier on, needing to get it all out before I give into him completely. "You don't know that. Everything's happening so quickly with us riding this wave of chemistry, but what about when things settle? You're a New York club owner with a vacation home in the town I plan on living in for at least a year. You're used to sophisticated women. Women with experience, and I'm not just talking in the bedroom. I mean women with connections, who can help you network."

"Brooke..." He sighs, and a softness enters his eyes. "I don't need a partner to help me grow my business. I've spent almost two decades doing it myself. What I need is a partner who sees me as I am. Just the man, not the CEO. Someone I can be myself with—even if it happens to be a possessive caveman." Travis winks, drawing a small smile from me. "What I need is *you*."

Sincerity rings throughout his voice and body. Hope, too. And I finally let myself melt into his embrace.

"Okay... so, we're doing this," I confirm, then glancing behind me, I can't resist teasing him. "And near a bed again. We're definitely improving our time and place."

A swift swat to my ass follows before Travis promptly throws me on the bed like I'm one of those tiny women who are easily pinned against walls and mattresses for sex.

And I guess for him I am.

"Oh, we're improving alright." He crawls up my body, dealing with each item of clothing he runs into by tearing it away. "Now I'm free to fuck you again without distraction. We're the only ones here, and I plan to take complete advantage of it and you. Because this weekend wasn't nearly enough. No amount of time will be enough."

Spreading my arms and legs out like a starfish, a wide, goofy grin lights me up from the inside out. "Do your worst, Mr. Gibson. I'm all yours."

Travis reaches my lips and stares down at me for a second, amusement darkening his eyes. "That's what I was hoping you'd say."

EPILOGUE ONE

TRAVIS

"I have roots when I doubted it would ever happen for me."

"I HAVE A FAVOR TO ASK." Brooke slides in next to me on the sofa and stares up at me with doe eyes. As if I could ever deny her anything.

"Consider it done."

She giggles and pokes my chest. "You don't even know what it is yet."

"Doesn't matter. If it's within my power to do so, then it'll get done." Brooke is my life. I love her with all my heart and soul, so whatever she needs, she'll get it.

It's that simple.

"It's Hope. She doesn't feel comfortable meeting everyone at the ranch yet, so I was wondering if she could stay here instead. Especially since the house will be empty with us gone."

The international side of my company needs attention, so Brooke is accompanying me on an eight-week business trip/ vacation. We've spent most of our time in Guardian Valley—I work remotely from my office while she writes in the sunroom, soaking in the beautiful scenery for inspiration. There's been the occasional trip back to New York, but Montana is our home now.

The year stipulated in Foster's will doesn't factor into our decision much, since we already decided to stay full-time in Guardian Valley. It's the perfect town to raise a family once we make that leap, and we've become close friends with the other Foster heirs.

I have roots when I doubted it would ever happen to me. Sure, I had friends in New York, but they were mostly business connections. Here, Derek, Heath, and even Winters don't give a damn about my clubs or my pedigree.

I don't have to smooth over the fact that I grew up in a trailer park with barely any money. Superficial things like that don't matter to them.

"Of course she can stay here, although you don't need my permission. This is your home, too. I'll let Braden know someone will be on the property," I say, although he's supposed to be handling a new club opening in Los Angeles this month and shouldn't be in Guardian Valley.

He's keeping his distance anyway after I told him to lay off Winters. Braden said he would, but he can be a bulldog when he wants something, and apparently, Harper's Landing is something he wants.

Which really fucks up any potential friendship with Winters. The man still pins me with suspicious glares during shared Sunday dinners at Serenity Ranch.

Braden needs to stop being a persistent ass.

"Thank you! I'll call Hope to let her know it's okay." Brooke kisses me then hops off the couch. "Then I've got to finish packing. I can't believe we leave for London in two days!"

Her excitement is catching. It'll be fun showing her around Europe and then Asia, sharing her joy in places my jaded heart had long ago deemed old hat.

"Don't forget to pack my favorite dress. You know the one." It's the dress she wore when we first met, the slinky number that first caught my eye and drew me to the love of my life.

She rolls her eyes. "Have I ever forgotten it during one of our trips?"

No, she hasn't.

Other couples may have songs or movies, but we have that dress. No matter how often she wears it, it's special.

I'll probably be eighty years old and seeing her wear that sexy number will get a rise out of my cock. Smiling at the thought, I watch her saunter upstairs.

Can't wait.

EPILOGUE TWO

BROOKE

"My perfect romance hero come to life."

"YOU'LL BE WORKING WHERE?" My brother and I are lounging on the deck while Travis lets us catch up. Ryan flew in from New York late last night after wrapping up his final contractual obligation before retiring from his professional hockey team.

I expected today to be spent discussing what he wants to do next, not for him to arrive with a plan already in motion.

"Not you, too." Ryan sighs and lets his head fall back on the Adirondack chair with a thump, the brim of his baseball cap shifting to shadow his face more. "Jason thought it was a step backward in my career, too, but I don't care. It's not like I need the money, especially with what Foster left us."

Jason is, or *was*, Ryan's sports agent. I could see why he'd be concerned about this new direction his client is taking.

High school hockey coaches don't land wealthy sponsors. They don't incite pandemonium among sports fans. Don't sign huge contracts where an agent would receive a large percentage of the profits.

"That's not it. I just never imagined you coaching teenagers. What about that broadcasting position with ESPN?" He'd mentioned the offer after releasing his retirement announcement.

Ryan shrugs, his lips forming a thin line. "I did a trial run last week. It's not for me. I'm not cut out for business suits and talking about player stats and highlight reels. Just because I'm a retired player doesn't mean I want to stay off the ice."

"When I researched Guardian Valley online, the job listing popped up, and it seemed like kismet. The principal was only too happy to offer the position. Guess hockey's a big thing around here, but since the old coach passed away six years ago, they've struggled to return to the championship level they used to be at."

"Wow... You're serious about this."

Ryan shoots me a sheepish grin. "Yeah. Playing professionally was never going to last long-term, and now I feel like I can make a difference in these kids' lives."

"If anyone can, it's you." Warmth spreads in my chest at his conviction. My brother has always had a soft spot for children, ever since we lost our parents at such a young age.

He volunteers with Big Brothers Big Sisters.

Plays Santa at charity events.

He's a good guy and deserves happiness. Even if it involves coaching a bunch of rowdy teens.

Travis walks out with a tray of snacks and bottles of water. "Sorry to interrupt, but you need to eat. You skipped breakfast." He stares pointedly at me, and I roll my eyes, though I'm secretly pleased with how attentive he is.

My perfect romance hero comes to life.

"Yeah, sis. Can't be skipping breakfast," Ryan taunts. He shares a brotherly nod with Travis, a smirk brightening his features.

I'm glad Ryan and Travis get along, but I don't care for them teaming up against me, not that it happens often. "Shut it," I mutter, reaching for a cracker and cheese. "Ryan is going to be the new head hockey coach at the high school."

"Congratulations." Travis takes that as his cue to sit next to me on the deck swing and slings an arm over my shoulders.

"Thanks, I'm looking forward to it."

"So, when do you start?"

Ryan grins and rubs his hands together like he's already concocting a plan for the season. "Our first game is late October, but we'll have tryouts for the team when school starts back up in August."

"Whoa, that's a few weeks away."

"Yup, which is why I want to have everything settled beforehand." Ryan stuffs a double-stacked cheese, turkey, and cracker sandwich in his mouth. "I'll meet with a realtor tomorrow about renting something closer to the school. The ranch is cool, but a little further out than I prefer if I'm going to be trekking back and forth between the high school and the ice rink."

"Well, if you need any help, let us know, and of course, you're welcome to stay here, though it's not much closer to town," Travis says as he toys with my hair.

Ryan's brows hit his hairline, and he vehemently shakes his head. "No offense, but I'm not too keen on hanging around you lovebirds all the time. There's only so much PDA a brother can take."

I laugh at his disgusted face. To mess with him, I twist to face Travis. "I don't know what he's talking about," I say with false innocence.

Travis catches on and leans closer. "I haven't a clue either." Then our lips touch in a searing connection. Ryan's groan in the background has me smiling into the kiss.

God, I love my life. Annoying my big brother and loving this man.

I couldn't have written a more perfect happily ever after for myself if I tried.

And I've gotten damn good at those, too.

Only two more heirs left! Don't miss Hope in *Montana Rescuer* and Ryan in *Montana Guardian*!

THANKS FOR READING & DON'T FORGET TO RATE/ REVIEW!

Please consider leaving a rating/review. Ratings & reviews are the #1 way to support an indie author like me.
The more reviews, the more my books are shown to other potential readers!
And they serve as guides to readers on whether or not to take a chance on an indie author.
I appreciate your support!
XO, Hallie

ABOUT THE AUTHOR

Hallie prefers steamy, insta-love stories where curvy girls are claimed by filthy-talking heroes. And when she ran out of reading material, she decided to write her own stories. If you want a quick, hot read, she's your girl!

Don't miss out on Hallie Bennett updates by joining her VIPs <u>here</u>[1]!

---

1. https://www.thearrowedheart.com/hallie-bennett

www.ingramcontent.com/pod-product-compliance
Lightning Source LLC
Chambersburg PA
CBHW030358180626
46812CB00007B/2937